Plain Jan ~~y.~~ **No,**
gorgeous

Her clothes ~~hair~~
fluffed arou ~~People she'd known her~~
whole life passed her on the street without a
flicker of recognition. Allison hadn't run into
Jeff yet, but he was due to pick her up soon. She
tried to corral the butterflies in her stomach.
Would he whistle with appreciation? Would he
stare with his mouth open? Would he take her
in his arms and kiss her passionately?

The doorbell rang. Allison held her breath and
opened the door.

"Hey, Allie." Jeff flashed an easy smile. "Are you
ready?"

"Um, yeah," she managed.

"I'll get these." He took her two bags to the car
and stashed them alongside his. "Hey, we have
matching bags."

Allison wasn't sure how she managed to
assemble words and phrases, but she must
have done all right, because Jeff didn't seem
to notice anything out of the ordinary.

And that was just the problem, wasn't it? She
had changed everything about her appearance.
And Dr. Jeff Hardison hadn't even noticed!

Dear Reader,

What a special lineup of love stories Harlequin American Romance has for you this month. Bestselling author Cathy Gillen Thacker continues her family saga, THE DEVERAUX LEGACY, with *His Marriage Bonus*. A confirmed bachelor ponders a marital merger with his business rival's daughter, and soon his much-guarded heart is in danger of a romantic takeover!

Next, a young woman attempts to catch the eye of her lifelong crush by undergoing a head-to-toe makeover in *Plain Jane's Plan*, the latest book in Kara Lennox's HOW TO MARRY A HARDISON miniseries. In *Courtship, Montana Style* by Charlotte Maclay, a sophisticated city slicker arrives on a handsome rancher's doorstep, seeking refuge with a baby in her arms. *The Rancher Wore Suits* by Rita Herron is the first book in TRADING PLACES, an exciting duo about identical twin brothers separated at birth who are reunited and decide to switch places to see what their lives might have been like.

Enjoy this month's offerings, and be sure to return each and every month to Harlequin American Romance!

Happy reading,

Melissa Jeglinski
Associate Senior Editor
Harlequin American Romance

PLAIN JANE'S PLAN
Kara Lennox

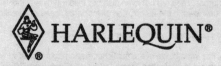

HARLEQUIN®

TORONTO • NEW YORK • LONDON
AMSTERDAM • PARIS • SYDNEY • HAMBURG
STOCKHOLM • ATHENS • TOKYO • MILAN • MADRID
PRAGUE • WARSAW • BUDAPEST • AUCKLAND

ISBN 0-373-16942-6

PLAIN JANE'S PLAN

Copyright © 2002 by Karen Leabo.

Visit us at www.eHarlequin.com

Printed in U.S.A.

ABOUT THE AUTHOR

Texas native Kara Lennox has been an art director, typesetter, advertising copywriter, textbook editor and reporter. She's worked in a boutique, a health club and has conducted telephone surveys. She's been an antiques dealer and briefly ran a clipping service. But no work has made her happier than writing romance novels.

When Kara isn't writing, she indulges in an ever-changing array of weird hobbies, from rock climbing to crystal digging. But her mind is never far from her stories. Just about anything can send her running to her computer to jot down a new idea for some future novel.

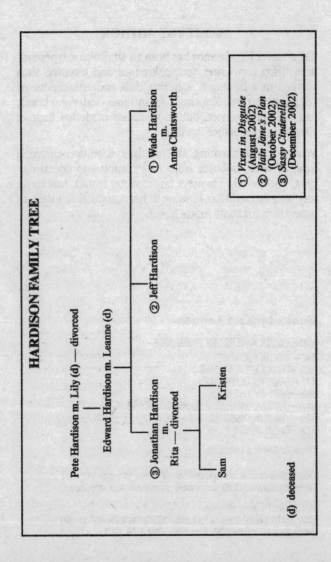

HARDISON FAMILY TREE

Pete Hardison m. Lily (d) — divorced

Edward Hardison m. Leanne (d)

③ Jonathan Hardison
m.
Rita — divorced

② Jeff Hardison

① Wade Hardison
m.
Anne Chatsworth

Sam   Kristen

(d) deceased

① *Vixen in Disguise*
   (August 2002)
② *Plain Jane's Plan*
   (October 2002)
③ *Sassy Cinderella*
   (December 2002)

Chapter One

"You *are* coming to the conference, aren't you, Jeffy?" the sultry female voice asked through Jeff's answering machine. "We had so much fun last year, and I just can't wait to see you again." The voice lowered to a sexy whisper. "I've got the most incredible new black dress. You'll love it. Okay, Jeffy? See you next weekend, bye-byeeeeee!"

Jeff Hardison groaned and flopped onto his leather sofa. He could almost see Sherry McCormick's frosted lips as she'd cooed her way through the message. Last year, at the medical products convention in Dallas, he'd found the man-crazy nurse an amusing distraction. But a little of Sherry went a long way, and he had no intention of spending four days with her stuck to him like a tick.

He briefly considered skipping the conference, but he really needed to go, since his father couldn't make it this year. Jeff and his dad prided themselves on having all the latest diagnostic equipment, despite the fact they ran a small-town medical practice in Cottonwood, Texas.

So how was he going to dodge Sherry? In fact, he'd just as soon dodge any female who had her sights on him. He was tired of shallow relationships with shallow women who saw a single doctor as their ticket to the country-club life. He was even a bit tired of the ones who just wanted to party.

A knock on his door distracted him momentarily from his dilemma. When he opened the door, he was pleased to see his friend Allison Crane on his porch.

His pleasure quickly turned to concern when he realized she had a bleeding elbow. A huge tear in the leg of her sweatpants revealed a nasty case of road rash along the side of her leg. Her bike was lying in the grass in his front yard with a bent wheel, telling the rest of the story.

"Hi, Jeff," she said quickly before he could express his concern. "I'm fine, don't worry, I just slid in a patch of gravel, hit a pothole, and got myself two flat tires. Since I was right up the street—" she shrugged "—I just want to use your phone."

Jeff dragged her inside. "Hell, Allie, you're going to kill yourself on that bike if you don't slow down."

"I wasn't going that fast," she protested as he led her into the kitchen. "Can I use your phone?"

"To call 911?"

She laughed. "I'm not hurt that badly, just a scratch. I was going to call Anne and see if she could run me and the bike home in her van."

In the kitchen, he took a piece of sterile gauze from the cabinet where he kept his first-aid supplies, then poured some antiseptic onto the gauze and faced Allison with a determined expression.

"Get away from me with that stuff. It stings."

"You can use my phone *after* you let me fix you up. God knows what kind of germs are lurking in gravel."

"Oh, you and your germs." But she capitulated, sitting in a chair at his kitchen table and rolling up the sleeve of her oversize T-shirt.

"I can give you a ride," he offered.

"That's not necess—ouch!" She jerked her arm out of his grasp when he tried to clean the cut on her elbow. "Surely medical science has invented a disinfectant that doesn't sting by now."

"Stop being a baby." After wiping away some of the blood, he inspected the cut more closely. "You're bleeding like Niagara Falls here. You need stitches."

"No way. I'll just apply pressure. It'll stop bleeding in a minute."

Jeff shook his head. "You are the most pigheaded person when it comes to medical care. You'd bleed to death before you let someone take a couple of stitches."

"Pigheaded! You're the one who hasn't seen a dentist in three years."

"My teeth are fine."

"And my elbow is fine. You and your needles can just keep away from me."

Despite her protests, he managed to clean out the cut to his satisfaction. The bleeding had already slowed. "All right, maybe some antibiotic ointment and a couple of butterfly bandages will do the trick," he said. "Can I at least do that?"

Allison frowned. "If it'll make you feel like a hero."

Jeff stifled the smile that threatened. Taking care of a patient, any patient, *always* made him feel like a hero. Most people thought he'd gone into medicine simply because his father was a doctor. But that had little to do with his career choice. In fact, he'd been planning a very different path, something related to business or marketing, leading to a fast-paced job and a corner office and all the big-city excitement he could handle. Then his mother had gotten sick, and he'd watched, helpless, as this doctor and that one tried futilely to save her.

Jeff's father, himself a physician, had accepted her death. He'd accepted the fact that medical science had limits, and he'd let his wife go, knowing he'd done his best. But Jeff hadn't let go so easily. He'd disappeared into the woods for hours, screaming at the unfairness of it all. Then he'd vowed that he would never be that helpless again. He would learn the healing arts, learn them better than anyone ever had, so no one he loved would get sick and die like that.

As he got older, he realized his outlook had been naive. Doctors weren't gods, and sometimes patients died. But he always took it hard when one of his patients slipped away. And he'd never gotten over the thrill of finding a cure, easing pain, giving comfort and occasionally pulling off something that bordered on miraculous.

He would never say it aloud, because it sounded so sanctimonious, but being a doctor truly was his calling.

ALLISON WINCED as Jeff deftly cleaned the scrapes on her leg.

He looked up with clear, blue eyes that could melt a glacier. "I'm sorry, did I hurt you?"

"It's okay," she said. It wasn't the pain that made every nerve ending in her body stand at attention. It was the touch of Jeff's hands on her bare skin. They'd played doctor once, when they were children, but ever since then she had assiduously avoided letting Jeff practice his medical arts on her. It wasn't that she mistrusted his skill. He was one of the best doctors in all of East Texas. But she was deathly afraid that if he touched her, her bodily reactions would give her away.

Thank goodness he thought her fidgeting and shortness of breath were due to discomfort, rather than the fact she was so hot and bothered she couldn't sit still.

She was crazy in love with Jeff Hardison, had been since she was thirteen. Unfortunately, Jeff had never given her any indication that he reciprocated, so she had pined away in secrecy. He'd always been a good friend to her—really, her best friend—but nothing more, and she would die a thousand deaths if he ever found out her true feelings.

She'd known since high school that he would never be the one for her. Jeff gravitated toward sophisticated females with style, panache and long legs. She had none of those things. Even losing sixty pounds—a result of her newfound passion for bicycling—hadn't turned her into the sort of femme fatale Jeff went for.

It was hopeless, completely hopeless. She never should have opened her dental practice back home in Cottonwood, where she saw him all the time. They hung out with each other. She even spent time with his family at the Hardison Ranch, which Jeff's brother Jonathan ran. She was constantly reminded of everything she couldn't have. Yet, a certain perverse part of her enjoyed being with him. It was torture, but sweet torture.

Jeff applied a couple of bandages over the worst scrapes on her legs. "There, that ought to keep you from bleeding all over my car."

"You don't have to take me home. Anyway, I couldn't fit a loaf of bread in the trunk of your Porsche, much less a bicycle."

"You can pick up the bike later. I trust you won't be riding it right away."

"Of course I will."

He gave her a disapproving frown.

"Oh, all right, you can take me home," she said. as if it were a great concession on her part. In truth, she loved riding in Jeff's luxurious, dark-green sports car, loved the buttery feel of his calfskin seats and the powerful purr of the engine, barely contained on the calm streets of Cottonwood. "I need to take the bike into the shop, anyway, to have that wheel straightened out."

She would ride her mountain bike until the racing bike was repaired, but Jeff didn't have to know that.

"That road rash will be a great topic of conversation next weekend," Jeff commented as they headed for his garage.

"Next weekend?"

"The convention? You're going, aren't you?"

"That's next weekend? Oh, shoot, I think I forgot to send my money in. I've probably got back-to-back patients next Thursday and Friday, too."

"Allie, you have to go."

She was surprised by the urgency in his voice. "Why?"

"Because it's no fun without you. Anyway, you have to save me from Sherry McCormick."

"That nurse with the curly blond hair?"

"That's the one. She's planning to hunt me down at the convention and make me her love slave."

Allison rolled her eyes. "The fact that you're irresistible to women is a curse you'll just have to live with. What's wrong with Sherry, anyway? I remember her from last year. She seems just your type."

"You really know how to hit below the belt."

"Well, if you want to discourage her attentions, wear a fake wedding ring. That ought to cool her jets."

Jeff opened the passenger door to his dark-green Porsche and helped Allison into her seat with more concern than usual. Allison enjoyed his solicitousness. She just wished it wasn't because she'd left half her skin in the intersection up the street.

"I doubt Sherry would be dissuaded by a wedding ring," he said as he slid behind the wheel. "She'd just consider it a little extra challenge. What I need is a wife, a flesh-and-blood wife."

Allison batted her eyelashes. "Why, Jeff, this is so sudden."

Jeff didn't laugh, as she expected he would. Instead he looked at her with a speculative gleam in his eye.

"What?"

"How would you like to be my fiancée for the weekend? Run a little interference for me?"

"I told you, I'm not going to the convention."

"You can change your plans. It's not too late to register as a walk-in. C'mon, Allie, it'll be fun."

Allison's instincts told her to say yes. What a fantasy, walking around for four days on Jeff Hardison's arm, pretending they were engaged. "It would be dishonest."

"It would save me from Sherry the Leech. Please?"

"What about all the other women? As I recall, you usually cut a wide swath on a long weekend in Dallas."

"Not this time. I'm mending my ways. No more tomcatting. I'll be your devoted fiancé, proper in every respect."

That would be the day.

"I'll take you to dinner at Antares," he wheedled.

Antares was the revolving restaurant atop Reunion Tower in downtown Dallas, and Jeff knew darn well it was her favorite restaurant. He was really going for the jugular.

She heaved a long-suffering sigh. "Let me see if I can rearrange my appointments." She knew all the while she would give in to his request. She was pretty much powerless to say no to Jeff, and he knew it. Anyway, she'd been looking for an excuse to get up to Dallas and see her former roommate, Stephanie Rich, who was a gynecologist. If she phoned right away, Steph could probably squeeze her into her schedule.

She most definitely did not want to see her regular doctor, who happened to be Jeff's father, about her little health problem.

ANNE HARDISON froze, a French fry halfway to her mouth. "You're going to do *what?*"

Allison enjoyed the look of shock on her friend's face. They were lunching at their usual spot, Triple Z Barbecue. Anne's husband, who was Jeff's younger brother, Wade, was taking his turn today watching their new baby.

"I'm going to pose as Jeff's fiancée to keep this certain woman, Sherry, from hitting on him at the convention," Allison explained. "She just about drove him crazy last year."

"And you agreed?" Anne asked, dumbfounded.

"Sure. Why not? It's a favor between friends.

Anyway, he promised to take me to Antares for dinner.''

"You could afford to take yourself to Antares. Allison, honey, he's taking advantage of you. He's *using* you.''

"Oh, he's not, either." Allison took a bite of her barbecued beef sandwich. She loved the fact she could eat anything she wanted, guilt-free, since she started bicycling.

"Yes, he is," Anne insisted. "He's a big boy, and I've seen him break a heart or two without blinking an eye. I'm sure he can fight off a dozen Sherrys if he wants to. I think he has another angle.''

"Like what?" Allison took a sip of iced tea.

"I don't know. Like…like maybe he's tired of being single, and he wants to test the waters—see how it might feel to be committed, without really committing.''

Allison laughed so loud the construction workers at the next table looked over. "That's the craziest thing I ever heard.''

"No, I think I'm on to something," Anne said, her enthusiasm rising in her voice. "Jeff has been hanging around at our place quite a bit, helping out with the rodeo camp. He's wonderful with the kids, and sometimes I catch him looking at Wade and me and the baby with this sort of wistful expression on his face.''

"You think he's jealous of your marital bliss?''

"All men get the urge to settle down and procreate sooner or later, even Jeff.''

Allison took a particularly savage bite of an onion ring. "Even if you're right, I'm not the one he fantasizes about. I mean, get real."

"What do you mean, 'get real'?"

"I mean, Jeff can have any woman he wants. Why would he set—"

"Don't you dare use that word, *settle*. Jeff Hardison would be damn lucky to have you. Any man would."

Allison rolled her eyes. "Yeah, yeah, yeah. Listen, Anne, you don't have to stroke my ego. Jeff is attracted to sophisticated model-types with long legs and collagen lips. We both know I'm no beauty queen."

Anne threw down her French fry, splattering ketchup on the checkered tablecloth. "That is such bull! You could go up against any woman in this town—or anywhere, for that matter. You've got great skin, great cheekbones, great hair—"

"Mousy brown is not great."

"But it's thick and shiny, and—"

"Anne, cut it out, okay? I don't care that Jeff doesn't notice me."

"Oh, don't you?" Anne asked innocently. The silence that followed her question was charged with enough tension to suffocate a mule.

"We're just friends, and I like it that way," Allison said, trying her best to sound casual.

"Liar."

Suddenly Allison found it hard to swallow. She'd nurtured her ridiculous crush on Jeff for years, and no one had ever suspected. Or had they? She'd never said a word to anyone and always acted completely indifferent around Jeff, but Anne was very observant.

"You haven't mentioned this to anyone, have you?" Allison asked, dying a thousand deaths. Her secret, her precious secret, was out in the open.

"Um, I don't know how to tell you this, but I don't have to mention it. Everyone knows."

Allison thought she was going to throw up. Surely this was just a terrible nightmare. "Everyone?"

"Everyone but Jeff, the lunkhead. I guess he's so used to women adoring him that he's oblivious."

Here, at least, was a shred of hope. "You're sure he doesn't know? And nobody's said anything to him?"

"Not that I've heard."

"Listen, Anne. He can never, never know. Promise me you won't say anything to Jeff."

"I won't. I wouldn't do that. But, Allison, why can't he know? In every relationship, someone has to make the first move. Why don't you just tell him how you—"

"I did that once."

"When? I thought—"

"In seventh grade. I screwed up my courage and asked him to the Christmas dance at the country club, and he was grossed out by the whole idea."

"Good Lord, Allie, that was eons ago. He probably doesn't even remember it."

"Well, I do." No sting of rejection had ever hurt so badly.

"You need to try again," Anne said gently.

"No! Oh, Anne, you don't know what you're saying." Allison scooted out of the booth. The restaurant suddenly felt stifling, suffocating. She had to get out. She threw a twenty-dollar bill on the table and scrambled to her feet, unable to get to the door fast enough.

"Allison, wait," Anne called, hot on her tail.

In the parking lot outside, Allison stopped and caught her breath. "Anne. I am not Jeff's type. If he knew I had...feelings for him, it would just make him uncomfortable, and then he'd feel sorry for me, and I can't be some object of pity, I just can't. I could never be friends with him again. At least if we're friends, I can see him."

"And slowly torture yourself to death. Allison, honey, that's no way to live."

"You have another suggestion? Besides making a total fool of myself? I'd have to move, you know. If he rejected me, I'd have to leave Cottonwood forever."

"Chill out, drama queen." Anne was walking slow circles around Allison, chin in hand, looking very thoughtful.

"What? Did I spill something on myself?"

"What if I could turn you into 'Jeff's type'?"

"Huh? You mean, like, a makeover?"

"Yeah. I'm not trying to hurt your feelings, Allison, but you don't exactly enhance your good points.''

''You mean because I don't wear two pounds of makeup and a push-up bra, and tease my hair like Dolly Parton? That's not me, Annie.''

''I'm not suggesting you do any such thing. But you hide your figure under baggy clothes, and you've been wearing the same hairstyle since junior high.''

''I'm comfortable with myself this way.''

''Yeah, because no one notices you. Believe me, I know what I'm talking about because I've been there. I was a nerdy law student before I met Wade, remember? Men never looked twice at me. But one crazy night I did myself up like a country-and-western singer and went to the rodeo, and boy, did the men notice.''

''One man in particular,'' Allison said with a smile, recalling Anne and Wade's tumultuous courtship. Anne had settled on an image that was somewhat toned down from the vampy rodeo queen. But Allison had to admit, her friend was a knockout now, when before she'd been easy to overlook. ''But *I'm* just not the girly-girl type,'' Allison added.

''You say you want Jeff to make the first move,'' Anne said, ''but he's never going to do that if he doesn't *notice* you.''

''I could walk down the street stark naked and he wouldn't notice. I lost sixty pounds—*sixty pounds*—and he never said a word.''

"That's because you're still wearing size sixteen clothes!"

Allison looked down at what she was wearing. "Am I that bad?"

"Frankly, yes! Let me play Professor Higgins. Maybe you'll like it. If not, there's nothing lost."

Allison sighed. "Okay, if you really want to. But it won't do any good."

"Maybe not. But there's a whole sea of men out there besides Jeff."

ALLISON PACKED and repacked her suitcase, making sure she had everything in her arsenal that she would need for the convention.

Three Miracle Bras in various colors, check.

Garter belt and stockings, check.

Catch-me-kiss-me, four-inch pumps, check.

Little black dress with no back, check.

Two pounds of makeup she'd sworn she wouldn't wear, but which made her look like a supermodel so she'd changed her mind, check.

Clingy tops two sizes too small, and pants that showed her belly-button, check.

Dangly jewelry, check.

Contraceptive devices—like she would need them—check.

As she zipped the suitcase closed, she caught a glimpse of herself in the dresser mirror, and her heart skittered around until she realized there wasn't a stranger in her bedroom. Anne had done a real number on her. They'd taken two evenings to accomplish the makeover, plus an evening of shopping, but the results were more than Allison had ever dreamed of.

Plain-Jane Allison was now pretty. No, she was gorgeous. A knockout. She hardly resembled the creature she'd been before. Her clothes were stylish and figure revealing, and her figure was worth revealing, taut as a bowstring but still softly curved. Her makeup enhanced her dark eyes, full lips, and sharp cheekbones.

And her hair—that was the wildest change. Anne had taken her to her favorite stylist, who had suggested golden highlights and a feathery cut that fluffed around her face. Jeez, she was almost a blonde.

People she'd known her whole life passed her on the street without a flicker of recognition. Her own patients stared at her as if she was going topless. And her parents…well, they'd been surprised to say the least. Her father, a church minister, had actually given her a brief lecture on the sins of the flesh. Her mother had nodded in agreement, then taken her aside and said, "Don't listen to your father. He's being a fuddy-duddy. You look fabulous. Do you think Anne might have time to show me how to do *my* makeup?"

Allison hadn't run into Jeff yet, but that would soon be remedied. He was due to pick her up any minute. They were riding together to Dallas, of course, as an "engaged" couple should.

Allison tried to corral the butterflies in her stomach. How would Jeff react to the new Allison, all decked out in low-cut jeans and a snug purple crop top? Would he whistle with appreciation? Would he stare with his mouth gaping open? Would he take her in his arms and kiss her passionately?

Well, okay, that third possibility was a pretty far-out fantasy. But she couldn't wait to see what he *would* do.

The doorbell rang and the butterflies fluttered themselves into a frenzy. This was it, her moment of truth. If *this* didn't prod Jeff into thinking of her as a desirable woman, she didn't know what would.

She hoisted her suitcase off the bed and wheeled it to the door, where her smaller bag of toiletries was already waiting. "Coming!" she called as she found her purse, a sassy little faux-alligator bag Anne had picked out for her.

Then she held her breath and opened the door.

Oh, Lord, he looked good. But then, he always did. Even as a skinny high-schooler, his broad shoulders and burgeoning muscles had hinted of good things to come.

"Hey, Allie." He flashed an easy smile. "Are you ready?"

"Um, yeah," she managed, searching for telltale signs of shock on his face. But he looked perfectly passive.

He spotted her two bags and reached for them. "I'll get these." He loped back out to his car, popped the trunk with a button on his key chain and stashed her luggage alongside his. "Hey, we have matching bags."

"Bought mine on sale at the outlet mall." She wasn't sure how she managed to assemble words and phrases into coherent sentences, but she must have been doing all right, because Jeff didn't notice anything out of the ordinary.

And that was just the problem, wasn't it? she thought with a wave of despair. Her big plan was a big, fat failure. She had changed *everything* about her appearance, and Dr. Jeff Hardison didn't even notice.

Chapter Two

Jeff drove along the interstate toward Dallas feeling inexplicably happy. He didn't particularly enjoy conventions. He wasn't big on strange hotel beds and banquet food. But he hadn't been out of Cottonwood for a while, and he supposed the idea of getting away for a few days was appealing.

The weather was fine, so he'd put the top down, enjoying the feel of the fall wind in his hair.

Allison didn't talk much. Before he'd lowered the convertible top, she'd put on a scarf to protect her hair from the wind and sunglasses to shield her eyes. Now she sat slouched in the passenger seat with a slightly petulant frown, lost in her own thoughts.

That was okay. It was hard to talk with all that wind. One thing he liked about Allison was that he didn't always feel obligated to carry on a conversation. She was comfortable with silence sometimes.

Maybe he shouldn't have pressured her into coming with him to Dallas. He probably could have dealt with Sherry some other way. But he was really glad Allison had capitulated. He would have someone to talk to among the sea of strangers, someone to eat meals with and rescue him from boring conversations. Allison could be counted on to ask provocative questions during tedious workshops or volunteer as a guinea pig when a vendor wanted to demonstrate a product.

He looked forward to seeing some old friends at the convention, fellow physicians who came every year basically as an excuse to play golf and escape their wives or girlfriends. He *didn't* look forward to announcing his "engagement" to them, though. He was the last holdout, and they would give him a hard time. But if he told them the engagement was fake, and the news leaked out to Sherry, she might know he'd carried out the deception to discourage her, and her feelings would be hurt...for about thirty seconds, before she sank her claws into him.

When he pulled up in front of the Del Mar Hotel, a valet scurried to open his door while a bellman did the same for Allison, then pounced on the bags. That was one drawback to driving a Porsche: everyone assumed you'd be a big tipper.

He didn't disappoint either man. Then he joined Allison by the revolving door and guided her inside with a hand at the small of her back.

Her bare back. Low-cut jeans and a crop top left her midriff bare. Funny, he couldn't recall ever seeing Allison's midsection before. Even when she rode her bike, she wore baggy shorts or sweats and oversize T-shirts.

He pulled his hand away, feeling sort of weird

about touching Allison. She was like a sister to him. Of course, if they were going to fool anyone into believing they were engaged, he would have to stifle any brotherly feelings and summon up some fake sexual sparks. He would have to get used to touching her.

The check-in desk was swamped with conventioneers. Jeff resigned himself to standing in line for a while. "You can go sit down if you want," he said to Allison. "I'll handle check-in."

"No, that's all right," she said coolly. "I've been sitting for three hours. Do you think they have a health club here?"

"It's a big hotel. I'm sure they do."

"Good. I missed my usual ride this morning, so I'd like to make it up on the stationary bike."

"Do you ride every day?"

"Six days a week. I'm training for a century next month."

"Century?"

"A hundred-mile ride."

Damn. He was in pretty good shape, and there was no way *he* could ride a bike for a hundred miles. Not unless someone gave him a week to do it. Since when had Allison become a jock? He seemed to recall that in a high school gym class she'd once hidden in the bushes to avoid being chosen for a softball team.

"Speaking of riding, how's the elbow?" he asked her. "And the road rash?"

"All better." She showed him her elbow, which

sported a fading bruise and just a thin scab. "I'm a fast healer. Oh, Jeff, I think that woman is trying to get your attention."

Jeff tensed, thinking it might be Sherry. But then he realized Allison was nodding toward one of the hotel clerks, who had just opened up a new station. She was looking straight at Jeff and motioning him to come be the first in her line, even though there were half a dozen people ahead of him.

Not one to look a gift horse in the mouth, he waltzed up to the desk.

"Hi, Dr. Hardison," the bouncy clerk said.

"How did you—"

"I checked you in last year, remember? You requested feather pillows and a standing wake-up call for 6:00 a.m."

Jeff was flabbergasted. "How do you remember that? You must check in fifty people a day, if not more."

"Yeah, but none of them are as good-looking as you," she said with an unmistakable come-hither look.

Oh, yeah. He remembered her now—remembered that beehive of bright red hair and the china-doll face.

"I have you down for the two-room suite with…oh, with a Ms. Allison Crane." She blushed.

"Dr. Crane," Allison said, setting her credit card on the desk.

Jeff scooped up the card and handed it back to her. "I'll get this…darling."

Allison's skin prickled with awareness as the *darling* sank in. How many times had she fantasized that word coming out of Jeff's mouth, those blue eyes looking at her with adoration, just as they were now?

This game they were playing was a mistake. She'd known that going in, known that deception of any kind always got her in trouble. But she'd done it anyway, because she'd thought pretending to be engaged might be fun. She hadn't counted on Jeff being such a good actor, producing these unwanted effects in her.

The clerk looked mortified over her faux pas. "I'm sorry, ma'am. Doctor. Doctor Crane. I wouldn't have been…I didn't know he was—"

"Engaged," Jeff said smoothly. "Allison is my fiancée."

The clerk found a smile. "How lovely. May I see your ring?"

Allison looked up at Jeff, slightly panicked. "Um, I don't have—"

"We're planning to shop for a ring while we're in the city," Jeff said. "We don't really have a good jewelry store selection in our hometown. Cottonwood is pretty small."

Allison hadn't realized Jeff could be such a smooth liar.

"You'll have to show me the rock when you get it," the clerk said to Allison with a wink as she handed each of them an electronic key, having apparently overcome her embarrassment. "I love diamonds."

"I'll bet you do," Allison murmured, then immediately felt guilty for being so catty. The clerk was just being friendly, and Allison could hardly blame her for flirting.

"You're in Suite 1516. If you'll point out your bags, I'll have the bellman bring them up."

Jeff gestured toward their matching suitcases, then casually slung an arm around Allison's shoulders and guided her to the elevator. The clerk watched them walk away, her eyes downright misty, before turning her attention to the next person in line.

"Well, wasn't that sweet," Allison said, stepping out of Jeff's light embrace the moment the elevator doors closed. She hoped he didn't notice her accelerated breathing, or the fact that beads of sweat had broken out on her forehead. "Is that how it is for you all the time? Women throwing themselves at your feet?"

"No, of course not. Some women just like to flirt. She's probably saying the exact same thing to the next person she checks in."

"Oh, I don't think so. She remembered you."

Jeff shrugged. "Some women have a thing for doctors. Anyway, getting hit on is a problem women have more than men, I think."

Not me, she wanted to add, because it was true. She couldn't remember the last time she'd had to fend off an unwanted advance. Maybe it was Hughey Jobson, in sixth grade, who'd threatened to kiss her on the mouth if she didn't hand over her Twinkies from lunch. But pointing that out would only gain Jeff's sympathy, not his passion.

"Well, anyway," she said, "I wish you would warn me next time before you present me as your fiancée. I wasn't ready."

"I thought we needed the practice."

"I'm supposed to protect you from Sherry. I didn't know I'd have to smile and simper for everybody."

"No one said anything about smiling and simpering. Jeez, that's not the kind of woman you think I'd marry, is it?"

"I can't see you marrying anyone."

He leaned against the elevator wall and folded his arms. "Why is that?"

"You're too fickle." She folded her own arms, mirroring his posture. "You buy a new car every six months. You throw out milk before the expiration date, and you won't eat a banana if it has a single brown spot. You have no tolerance for imperfection. Every woman you date has some fault—this one has an annoying laugh, that one has too many cats. You look for excuses to dump them. When you're married, you have to accept a person, faults and all. You have to *commit*. You can't just walk away when you get a little bit bored, or when something else attracts you.

"*That* is why I can't see you married."

Jeff just stared at her. Even when the elevator

doors opened onto their floor, he still stood there, his mouth slightly open, his eyes glazed.

Belatedly Allison realized she'd been too blunt. He'd been looking for a little harmless banter, and she'd given him a no-holds-barred assessment of his personality. She hadn't painted a very pretty picture.

"Well, thanks, Allison, for answering my question so…honestly." He walked off the elevator ahead of her.

Allison felt just awful. Jeff was her friend, one of her very, very best friends. Just because women threw themselves at him was no reason for her to launch such a personal attack toward him. He'd done nothing to her. She supposed her doctor's appointment with Stephanie tomorrow had her more on edge than she realized, and she was taking it out on poor Jeff.

She hurried down the hall after him. "Jeff, wait. I'm sorry."

He said nothing, just kept walking until he reached Suite 1516. He opened the lock with his electronic key, then threw the door open and gestured for her to enter.

When she saw the room, she was momentarily distracted from her need to apologize. The suite was gorgeous, the most luxurious space she'd ever seen. She'd never traveled much, and when she did, she stayed in a budget-minded place. It had taken her many years to pay off the huge debts from dental school, then the equipment she needed for her practice. She was out of debt now, but still didn't like to spend money wantonly. Last year when she'd attended this convention, she'd stayed at a Motel Six.

Jeff's financial situation was a lot different. His father had paid for med school, then welcomed him into the practice—where the equipment was already paid off.

"Wow." She wandered from the living room into the bedroom, resisting the urge to kick off her shoes and run barefoot through the inch-thick carpet. "This place must be costing you a fortune," she said. "Why don't we split the bill?" Even split in two, the rate would be three times what she normally paid, but it wasn't fair to make Jeff carry the whole burden, even if this engagement scheme was his idea.

"I can afford it," he said gruffly.

The bellman arrived moments later with their bags. He set them both up on luggage racks in the bedroom. Allison looked at those matching suitcases, side by side, and thought how cozy they must appear to the bellman.

Jeff tipped the man and sent him on his way. Then he wasted no time grabbing his suitcase and carrying it out into the living area. "You can have this room. I'll sleep on the fold-out sofa."

"You mean there's not a second bedroom?"

"No, this is it."

"I don't mind sleeping on the sofa. I'm smaller." She was proud of the fact she could say that and mean it.

"I'll try it first," he said. "But I probably won't

be able to *commit* to the sofa bed. I'll find lumps, or it'll sag in the middle—"

"Jeff…"

"And then I'll want to toss it aside and go for the king-size bed. C'mon, you know it's true."

"I was completely out of line with those comments, and I'm sorry." She stood in the bedroom doorway, talking to his back as he hoisted his bag onto the sofa and unzipped it. "Truly, Jeff. Can you forget I said them?"

He straightened, then slowly turned, a troubled frown marring his handsome face. "I'll always forgive you, you know that. But I can't forget. Is that how you actually see me? I had no idea."

"I was exaggerating. I was irritated because that beautiful woman threw herself at you, and you took it for granted. I was jealous."

"Jealous?" He stopped scowling at her.

"Yeah. Because beautiful men never throw themselves at me. It hardly seems fair." All right, so she was playing her sympathy ticket. Not very commendable, but if she could nudge Jeff out of his pique, she swore she would watch her tongue in the future. He might not see her "that way," but he was her friend and he cared for her, which gave her the power to hurt him. She'd never realized that before.

He finally smiled. "You'll find your white knight someday, Allie." Then he paused, looking thoughtful. "Do I really throw out perfectly good bananas?"

"I saw you do it once. And the—" She censored herself.

"The what?"

"Nothing."

"What, Allison? Tell me, or I'll tickle you."

Oh, no, not the tickle monster. He hadn't done that to her since junior high, when the mere thought of his perfect hands on the rolls of fat around her middle had prompted her to capitulate immediately to the threat.

Now, the idea of his hands on her ribs—no more rolls of fat—was unsettling for a different reason. Her hormones were already on red alert from the casual way he'd touched her in front of the hotel clerk. She couldn't handle any more touching at the moment.

She took an instinctive step backward. "I was going to say, 'And the heels from bread.' You throw those away, too."

"That has nothing to do with commitment. I never commit to the heels, even at the grocery store when I first put the bread in my basket. I always tell them up front, 'I'm not eating you. You're too tough.'"

She laughed, relieved he was no longer angry. "The heels make good toast. It's wasteful to toss them."

"I'll save all my heels for you. Okay, Miss Conservation?"

"Then you'll have to toast them for me for breakfast." *Oh, stop it.* She was flirting with him. What if he got completely turned off? What if he said,

Allison, there's no need to play the part of my lover when we're alone. It weirds me out.

But he didn't say anything. In fact, he didn't appear to even realize she'd dropped a provocative line.

While Jeff unpacked, she ogled the blindingly white-tiled bathroom with its Jacuzzi tub. She heard him opening and closing drawers in the living room. She'd decided not to argue further about his choice of bed. After all, if things worked out as she hoped, they'd get to *share* the big bed.

"We have just enough time to grab lunch before registration," he said after they'd both hung up their clothes and stashed toiletries in the bathroom. "There's a good sandwich place up the block."

Allison remembered the place. They served sandwiches as big as her head, along with piles of greasy potato chips and chocolate brownies to die for. Since she wouldn't be bicycling during the convention, she couldn't afford all those fat grams. "I think I'll check out the health club instead."

He looked at her curiously. He was probably remembering the old Allison, who never turned down a meal and thought walking to the refrigerator was plenty of exercise. Then he shrugged. "Suit yourself. I'll wait for you at registration."

He took off without much fanfare, and Allison slumped with disappointment. She'd been hoping Jeff would want to work out with her. There was no way he could fail to notice her newly sculpted body if she was wearing her skimpy new exercise clothes.

Or maybe he could. Sometimes she thought she must be invisible to Jeff.

Allison spent forty-five minutes on the exercise bike, another fifteen with free weights, then bought a strawberry-banana concoction and a cucumber sandwich at the juice bar. That would hold her to dinner. She showered, changed clothes, went to registration and signed up as a walk-in. She didn't see Jeff anywhere. So much for his promise to behave like a devoted fiancé.

Unfortunately, she did see Sherry. Or, more to the point, Sherry saw her. The buxom nurse, with her cloud of blond curls and black-lined eyes, marched up to Allison and hugged her as if they were long-lost friends.

"Allison, right?"

"Yes," Allison said, straightening the jacket Sherry's hug had knocked askew. "And you're Sherry."

"You remembered! Of course, everybody remembers me. I seem to make an impression, for better or worse." She gave Allison a once-over. "New... hair?"

"New everything."

"You're a friend of Jeff Hardison's, right?" Sherry scanned the crowd, looking for her quarry.

Uh-oh. Allison was either going to have to lie, or mess up Jeff's carefully planned strategy. "Yes, we came together." There. That wasn't a lie, but it implied something more personal than "just friends."

"Well, wasn't that nice of him to let you tag along," Sherry said with an uncertain smile.

Allison silently critiqued Sherry's caps. She couldn't help it; professional hazard. Hers were good.

Sherry reapplied her coral lipstick. "Does he still have that Jaguar?"

"No, he has a Porsche."

Sherry's eyes sparkled. *Ka-ching!* "Well, where is he? I'm just dying to give him a big ol' long-time-no-see kiss. He's such a doll."

Allison knew she had to say something. No self-respecting fiancée would allow this woman to kiss her future husband without protest.

"Um, maybe you better re-think your strategy," Allison said. "Jeff is spoken for these days."

Sherry looked horrified. "No, say it isn't true. He's not married, is he?" She said the word *married* as though it had four letters.

"Engaged," Allison said.

Sherry relaxed. "Oh, is that all? Then he's still a free man in my book."

"Well, he's not in mine," Allison said sharply.

Sherry's face fell. "You? He's marrying *you?*"

"Incredible as it may seem."

"Oh. Gosh, I'm just mortified. Talk about making a fool— Well. I see. I hope it…works out. You're not one of those clinging vines who tries to keep her man from having female friends, I hope. Because Jeff and I have known each other for years."

"I have no control over Jeff's friends." Unfortunately. Because if she did, she'd stuff Miss D Cups into a taxi and send her back to whatever slime pit she crawled out of.

The strength of Allison's jealous reaction startled her. She'd always been a bit wistful over the Sherrys of the world, confident of their sexuality and bold. She'd never felt the green-eyed monster's claws dig in like this before.

Sherry flashed another broad smile. "Good. Because it's hard to keep a man if you put too many restrictions on him."

"I'll remember that."

Allison barely restrained herself from kicking Sherry in her swaying butt as she walked away.

JEFF WAS LATE getting back to the hotel for registration. He'd run into an old friend in the lobby and lost track of the time. He looked around for Allison, but realized she must have come and gone already. She was planning to attend some seminars this afternoon, so she'd probably already gone to get a seat.

As he waited for the woman behind the registration desk to check him in, he heard a familiar laugh, and a cold chill washed over him. Sherry. He hadn't wanted to run into her without Allison on his arm, ready to back up his engagement story.

The registration woman seemed to be moving in slow motion. Finally she handed him his badge and packet. He grabbed them and turned, intending to hightail it to the elevator. Instead he ran smack into Sherry.

"Jeffy! I knew you were lurking around here somewhere." She grabbed on to him and put a lip lock on him that would have done a vacuum cleaner proud. He pushed her away so forcefully she almost fell off her spike heels.

"Sherry. It's nice to see you, too, but there's something I have to tell you."

"Is it about your fiancée?"

That threw him. "You…know?"

"I ran into Allison a few minutes ago. She's…sweet. But you could have knocked me over with a feather when she said you two were getting married. I always got the feeling you weren't the marrying kind."

"Well, people change." Jeff wondered how much of Sherry's orange lipstick was smeared all over his face.

"She just doesn't seem your type," Sherry persisted.

"Why is that?"

"Well, she's so…sweet. I can't picture her being able to handle a tiger like you." Sherry made a noise, a sort of combination meow-purr.

"Believe me, I'm thoroughly tamed."

"A tiger can never be tamed. You can put a collar on him and make him jump through hoops, but the minute the trainer drops her guard…" She swiped the air with her hand, her coral talons curling like claws.

Jeff had had just about enough of this conversation. Was the woman not able to take a hint? "Yes, well, interesting observation. I have to go. Allison's waiting for me.'' He made his escape, finally breathing a sigh of relief when he reached the safety of the elevator.

None of the afternoon workshops appealed to him. He went for a swim in the hotel's Olympic-size pool, wishing he'd worked out with Allison instead. At least he'd have had someone to talk to, and he wouldn't have that pastrami sandwich sitting in his stomach like a lump. He sat in the whirlpool for a while. The only other person there was a woman from Albuquerque, a bookkeeper for a medical clinic who was attending the conference to brush up on the latest insurance laws. Jeff steeled himself for a come-on, but then she started talking about her husband and daughter, and he realized she was just being friendly, not flirting.

Not all women threw themselves at him, as Allison believed. Hell, he'd been turned down by plenty of 'em. He could remember times he'd been ignored and overlooked by the opposite sex. She didn't have a corner on that market.

Come to think of it, though, he couldn't remember Allison ever dating anyone. Maybe he should set her up with a nice guy. He had a few single friends left.

That thought immediately made him uneasy. No, he wouldn't meddle in Allison's love life. That was a sure way to ruin a perfectly good friendship—introduce her to some guy who later dumps her, and then Jeff would take the blame.

When he glanced at the clock, he realized he

ought to go to the suite and change for the reception. He hoped Allison was there, so they could go together. He didn't want to face Sherry again without her.

ALLISON WAS READY a half-hour early. Her new hairdo and makeup routine took forever, so she'd left herself plenty of time. But it was only four-thirty, and the reception didn't start till five.

And where was Jeff? That thought had scarcely formed before she heard him at the door. Oh, shoot, she didn't want him to see her yet. He would know how eager she was, and besides, she wanted to make an entrance. She quickly retreated to her bedroom and closed the door.

"Allison? You here?"

"I'm getting dressed," she called through the closed door. "Bathroom's all yours."

"Thanks. Oh, and thanks for running interference with Sherry. You did good."

"No charge." She hoped they could steer clear of Sherry from now on. Lying didn't sit well with Allison.

With time to kill, she decided to polish her nails and tried not to think about the fact that Jeff was naked in the shower. Then she would get all hot and bothered, and her face would glow and her hair would go flat, and she would chew off her lipstick.

The water in the bathroom stopped, and she heard Jeff moving around in the living room. Probably getting dressed. Maybe she could walk in by mistake and catch him half-naked.

Oh, Allison, you are sick.

When her nails were dry and she judged she'd given him plenty of time to make himself decent, she doused herself with perfume guaranteed to drive any man wild, grabbed her tiny evening bag, and opened the door, walking with as much sensuous grace as she could manage.

Apparently, that wasn't very much, because the first thing she did when she entered the living area was trip.

Somehow, Jeff caught her before she hit the carpet face first. "Whoa. You all right?"

Just dying of embarrassment. "Fine, fine. New shoes. I'm not used to them."

He inspected her four-inch heels, then *tsked* at her. "Do you know how many women I've had in my office who have sprained their ankles wearing ridiculous shoes like that?"

"Don't lecture me, Jeff. I happen to like these shoes. Anne picked them out for me." She figured mentioning Anne couldn't hurt, since she was only slightly less revered than a saint in the Hardison family.

"I'll have to have a talk with her." He sneezed. "Are you wearing perfume?"

"Uh-huh."

"I think I'm allergic. What is that stuff?"

She would die before she admitted it was something called Seduction. "Mmm, I don't remember."

"Could you tone it down a little? I have to hang out with you all night."

Her face burning, Allison retreated to the bathroom. So, he thought hanging out with her was a chore, did he? She swiped her wrists, behind her ears, and between her breasts with a damp washcloth. The beast! He hadn't even noticed her dress, which had cost her two root canals and one crown. It was a sexy little black thing with a plunging neckline and no back and a hem much higher up her thigh than she'd ever worn before. And he hadn't said a word.

She said nothing as they rode down the elevator together. She wished he didn't look so damn handsome in his suit. She wished she could find something wrong with his appearance—some evidence that he was turning prematurely gray or thickening around the middle. But no such luck. He was more handsome than ever, and at the moment she *hated* him.

As soon as they arrived at the reception, which was packed with conventioneers eager to take advantage of the complimentary hors d'oeuvres, she excused herself to the rest room. In the ladies' lounge, she pulled out her cell phone and dialed Anne's number.

"Allison? What are you doing calling me? You're supposed to be seducing Jeff."

"It's not working. He said my shoes were stupid, my perfume stinks—"

"What about the dress?"

"It could have been a potato sack for all he noticed. I might as well be a piece of furniture."

"Why don't you pretend to trip and let him catch—"

"Been there, done that. He patted me on the shoulder like I was a golden retriever."

"This calls for drastic action. You've got to shake that boy up—but good."

"How?" Allison wailed. "I've tried everything."

"I bet you haven't kissed him."

Chapter Three

I bet you haven't kissed him.

Yeah, right, Allison thought as she minced her way back to the ballroom in her high heels. What was she supposed to do, just grab him and put a lip lock on him? Just give him a big ol' long-time-no-see kiss, like Sherry had wanted to do?

A woman like Sherry could get away with such behavior. If Allison tried it, though, Jeff would probably have her committed. Allison shook her head. She needed a plan, but a full frontal assault wasn't it.

Allison didn't immediately spot Jeff when she returned to the ballroom, which made her a bit uneasy. She wasn't a social butterfly, certainly no good at making small talk with strangers. She usually did her best imitation of wallpaper at these receptions and beat a hasty retreat as soon as she'd scammed some free hors d'oeuvres.

She was about to decide to do just that when she spotted Sherry, wearing a black halter dress with a plunging neckline. Allison supposed she ought to find her "fiancé" and live up to her end of the bad deal she'd made.

Maybe he'd gone to get them drinks at one of the crowded bars set up at either end of the ballroom. But a quick tour of lines of conventioneers waiting to order their beverage of choice didn't turn him up.

She was starting to feel a bit piqued that Jeff hadn't stayed where she'd left him. She reconsidered her urge to flee to the room and order room service, never mind they were supposed to go out to dinner at Antares, when a group of three men walked straight up to her.

"Allison?" the tallest one greeted her.

"Yes? Oh, Tom, how nice to see you again," she said, recovering quickly as she recalled his name. He was a dermatologist from Cincinnati with wavy black hair and killer brown eyes. She'd played match-stick poker with him in the lobby last year.

"I almost didn't recognize you. You've... changed something."

"I've changed everything," she said with a laugh, gratified that at least *this* man had noticed. "Whole new lifestyle."

"You look great." Those velvety brown eyes held hers just a trifle too long before he introduced her to his two friends, also dermatologists.

The two friends, Greg and Ian, practically elbowed each other to shake her hand first. Then they all stood in a semicircle around her and showered her with compliments and all kinds of attention.

Allison was overwhelmed. These men were *flirt-*

ing with her, and she hadn't done a thing. Two other men wandered over, friends of Ian drawn in by the laughter. Allison did her best not to act like the shrinking violet she wanted to be, matching joke for joke, asking questions of the men to deflect attention away from herself. After a few minutes she forgot to be nervous and found she was actually enjoying herself.

This had never happened to her before. Normally, if she was included in a group of people, it was on the fringes, listening and maybe laughing, but never saying much, and certainly not the center of attention.

Was this phenomenon a result of her change in appearance? Or had the changes she'd made caused her to project more outward confidence?

"So, would you like to join me for dinner?" Tom asked. "Greg and Ian have plans with their wives, so I'm…at loose ends."

Allison, caught up in the flirtation, was on the verge of saying yes. Tom was a charmer. But a masculine voice behind her saved her the trouble of answering.

"She has plans."

Allison whirled around to see Jeff standing behind her, his usually pleasant face darkened with a scowl. He slid a possessive arm around her waist, obviously laying claim to his territory.

She cleared her throat. "Tom, I'm sure you remember Jeff Hardison. We're from the same—"

"We're engaged," Jeff said, relaxing slightly as

he shook the other men's hands. "I promised Allison dinner at Antares."

Tom took a step back. "Well, congratulations, you two. I guess I'll have to make other plans myself." The rest of the men slithered away until Jeff and Allison stood alone.

Allison couldn't think of a thing to say.

"Our reservation is at seven-thirty," Jeff said tightly. "We'd better go."

As they stood outside the hotel waiting for the valet to bring Jeff's car around, Allison finally found her tongue. "That was pretty rude."

Jeff immediately relaxed, a smile forming on his sensual lips. "That's all right, I forgive you."

"You forgive—what are you talking about? You're the one who was acting like some caveman, coming on all macho, speaking for me. What were you doing, marking your territory?"

Jeff's smile vanished. "I was playing the part we agreed to play. You, on the other hand, seemed to have forgotten I existed, flaunting yourself in front of those men like some...some..."

"Single woman?"

"You're not single, at least not for the moment. You're supposed to be engaged to me. It doesn't reflect very well on me if my fiancée is throwing herself at every man who walks by—"

"You have totally lost your mind. I was making pleasant conversation. Anyway, if you don't want me talking to other men, you could be a bit more attentive yourself. You disappeared while I was in the rest room.''

"Another ice age came and went while I was waiting for you. What were you *doing* in there?''

Allison abruptly lowered her voice. ''Ix-nay, shark warning, three o'clock.''

"What?''

"Sherry!'' Allison whispered. ''And she's heading this way.'' Allison knew she ought to let Jeff sink in his own macho pool—just blow the whistle on him right here and now. But then she wouldn't get dinner at Antares. At least, that was what she told herself.

"Well, hi, you two!'' Sherry greeted them, coming up between them and putting her arms around both of them. ''Where are you two lovebirds off to this evening?'' Her nose was practically twitching, trying to find a weakness she could sink her teeth into.

"Antares,'' Jeff said, suddenly turning into the devoted fiancé. ''It's one of Allison's favorite places.''

"I've never eaten there,'' Sherry said. ''I've heard it's wonderful, unless you have motion sickness. Personally, I just don't think my food would settle with the restaurant spinning circles that high up in the air. You don't have that problem, do you, Allison?'' She looked at Allison, all innocence.

"Um, no.''

"I get car sick just thinking about it. I'd order

something light if I were you. Well, you two have fun. That's my car.''

The valet had just delivered a red Firebird. Sherry disengaged herself from Jeff and sashayed to her car, where two other women joined her.

"Thank you," Jeff said under his breath.

"I'm not going to renege on our deal just because you're acting like a Neanderthal."

"Listen, if you want to go out to dinner with Tom What's-his-face, just say so. Seems Sherry's safely occupied for the evening."

"Oh, no, you're not weaseling out of our dinner," Allison said, doing her best to hide her hurt feelings. She'd been looking forward to this romantic dinner all week. Apparently, he wasn't. "I'm ordering the most expensive thing on the menu."

Despite her threats, Allison ordered a modest dinner. She kept thinking about what Sherry said about motion sickness. The restaurant's movement was so subtle you couldn't really feel it—unless you were thinking about it, which Allison was. The last thing she wanted to do was spoil the evening further by becoming nauseated.

So she ordered a chicken breast and picked at it, barely sipping at the expensive wine Jeff had ordered to accompany their meal.

But, really, could the evening be any more spoiled? She and Jeff had never fought like this before. Even though they eventually apologized to each other, and Allison admitted that she *had* been flirting, and Jeff admitted that he'd overreacted, the bloom was off the rose of this evening. The panoramic view could have been a dingy brick wall for all the attention Allison paid it, and the food might as well have been sawdust.

JEFF CRINGED when he saw the bill. He wouldn't have minded paying a sky-high price for an enjoyable evening. But dinner had been an ordeal to be survived.

He still felt angry, even though he and Allison had apologized and were talking. He couldn't bring himself to tease her, the way he usually did. Their conversation was stilted, almost forced. He'd never had trouble talking to Allison before.

They returned to the hotel and practically raced each other upstairs. She seemed as eager to end the evening as he was. She beat him to the door with her key already out, then scurried into the bedroom and closed the door.

When she opened it again, she was wrapped head-to-toe in one of the hotel's roomy terry cloth robes. Her hair was slicked back from her face with a stretchy headband.

For some reason, her appearance was reassuring. Jeff relaxed slightly. Allison seemed suddenly more like his friend, less like the fake fiancée she'd been pretending to be in public.

"I'm done in the bathroom," she announced.

He brushed his teeth and washed his face. When he came back out of the bathroom, Allison was sitting stiffly on the sofa, watching the news. She immediately stood.

"Guess I'll turn in."

"The wake-up call's for six," he reminded her. "It'll ring in your room. If that's too early, we can change it."

"No, that's fine. I want to work out. Good night." With that terse dismissal she retreated into the bedroom and closed the door.

Jeff found an extra blanket and pillow in a closet, then undressed and stretched out on the sofa. The sofa was large, so it wasn't terribly uncomfortable. He shouldn't have had any trouble falling asleep, especially after the glass of wine he'd drunk with dinner.

But sleep eluded him. He was as tense as a coiled spring, and he found himself checking the illuminated dial on his watch every five minutes or so, wondering how long before he could relax.

He'd never in his life had insomnia. Something he ate, maybe? He couldn't even *remember* what he'd eaten. All he could recall was staring covertly across the table at Allison, wanting to shake her.

Now that was just patently stupid. He'd never touched a woman in anger and he wasn't going to start with his best friend. But why in the world was he so mad at her? And he was still mad, there was no denying it.

The truth hit him like a truckload of concrete. He was jealous. All those men flirting with Allison had brought out every savage instinct in his reptilian brain. He'd wanted to challenge Tom to a duel, run him through for daring to look at Allison's breasts—which was exactly what the jerk had been doing.

He couldn't possibly be jealous—that was ridiculous. If he'd wanted to make a conquest out of Allison Crane, he would have done so by now.

Or…maybe not. He talked with Allison all the time, and she told him all kinds of personal things. But maybe not everything. Maybe she had a string of boyfriends he wasn't even aware of.

He'd just never thought about this before. Allison dating, going out with men. She was in her midthirties, close to his own age. She'd said she couldn't see him married, but he'd never even *thought* about Allison falling in love, marrying, having kids.

Now he did—and it filled him with the most awesomely uncomfortable pricklings.

It couldn't be jealousy, it just couldn't be. Brotherly protective instincts—that was it. All big brothers resisted the idea of their little sisters falling in love, getting married…having sex.

Relieved to have put a name to the strange phenomenon, Jeff was finally able to relax and fall asleep. But the next morning those foreign feelings assaulted him anew, stronger than ever.

He and Allison ordered a light room-service breakfast. The waiter set the food up at a small round table, and Jeff and Allison sat down to eat, both of them in their exercise clothes. Jeff's gaze was drawn again and again to Allison's breasts, revealed rather fetchingly in a clingy blue shirt.

No wonder Tom had stared.

Allison ignored him and read the paper, which was a good thing or she might have noticed his state of agitation. No, *agitation* wasn't the right word. *Arousal* said it better.

He couldn't believe it, but he could no longer deny it. He'd known her for twenty-five years or more. Why was he only now noticing how shapely Allison's legs were? How had he never noticed how alluring that hollow in her throat was? She drank a big glass of water with lemon to prepare for her workout, and he watched her lush lips wrap themselves around the straw as she took a sip. His arousal was going to be painfully evident when they stood up.

But no thoughts of cold showers or tax audits or Mrs. Simmonetti, his third-grade teacher, could douse his sudden ardor.

"I want to get going," he said abruptly. He sprang to his feet and bolted from the table before Allison even had a chance to look up. He grabbed his key and exited the room, hoping a couple of seven-minute miles might set everything aright.

Three miles into his run, he realized nothing would ever be the same now that he'd brushed up with the idea of sexual awareness of Allison Crane. He could never take the notion any further, of course. Allison wasn't the type of woman to trifle with, and he sure as hell wasn't in the market for a serious relationship—Allison had been right about his commitment aversion. Besides, Allison was his friend, really his best friend. Nothing messed up a friendship like sex.

That was assuming he could have sex with her if he wanted, which he seriously doubted. He'd seen the way she was flirting with those guys at the reception. She'd never acted like that with him.

And if those weren't reasons enough to put these ridiculous thoughts right out of his mind, there were a couple dozen people who would have his hide if he trifled with Allison, if he approached a relationship with her with anything but the utmost respect and the most serious of intentions. Respect he had, but serious intentions were out of the question. His sister-in-law, Anne, would have him drawn and quartered. She was a force to be reckoned with.

At least he'd come to a decision. He would not act on these newly hatched desires. He would ignore them, deny them and eventually conquer them.

He absolutely would not try to seduce Allison Crane.

ALLISON STARED at the door where Jeff had disappeared for a long time. What was with him? She couldn't imagine he was still angry after their stupid disagreement last night. He wasn't the type to hold a grudge, and everyone agreed he was the most easygoing of the three Hardison brothers.

She could only conclude that he just didn't want to be with her right now. Pretending to be her fiancée was more of an acting job than he'd counted on, and he couldn't take the pressure.

Well, what else could it be?

When Allison returned to the room after her workout, it appeared Jeff had already showered, dressed and cut out. Feeling disappointment mixed with relief, she dressed in one of her new outfits, a red knit dress with a zipper down the front. She couldn't afford to wear heels today, not when she had miles of convention floor to cover. She had to get as much done this morning as she could, because her doctor's appointment was scheduled for two o'clock.

She put on a pair of red Keds with lace socks.

Once on the trade show floor, Allison consulted her map and zeroed in on the vendors that interested her. She needed a new irrigation system for her office—the old one was so ancient it leaked all over her patients. And she wanted to find a new supplier for dental stone and X-ray blanks. The one she was using was woefully unreliable.

Shortly before lunch, she was pleased with the progress she'd made. She'd found a new irrigation system that she could actually afford, and she'd gotten a number of other dental supply companies to agree to come by her office and bring her free samples. She'd also filled up a canvas tote bag with freebies she could pass on to her patients—toothbrushes, toothpaste, flavored floss, whitening systems. What fun.

She'd also managed to stop thinking about Jeff, at least for a little while. Her plan to convince him she was a desirable woman, worthy of his romantic attention, was a bust, and she had almost come to

terms with the idea that she would have to extinguish
the flame she'd been carrying for him since junior
high and look elsewhere for male companionship.

Then she saw him, just before lunch, walking
down one of the aisles at a brisk pace—with Sherry
trotting after him like a loyal puppy.

Sherry was nothing if not determined.

Allison sighed. She supposed she ought to rescue
him. That was the deal, the price she paid for staying
in this nice hotel.

She caught up with him, pasting on a smile.
"There you are. I've been looking for you all morning."

Jeff smiled, too, an expression she hadn't seen on
his face since sometime yesterday. "This place is a
zoo."

"Are you ready for lunch?" she asked brightly,
taking his arm. It was a struggle, touching him and
acting as if it was nothing. She could feel the heat
of his skin through his shirtsleeve.

"Sure, let's go."

"Mind if I sit with y'all?" Sherry asked.

Jeff started to object, but Allison elbowed him.
"We'd love to have you." She didn't know why,
but suddenly she felt sorry for Sherry. After all,
Sherry was in the same boat as Allison, carrying a
torch for Jeff Hardison, who wasn't the least bit interested. Allison was sure Sherry wouldn't be a
problem at lunch, so long as Jeff's fiancée was there
to protect him.

At lunch they found themselves at a table with an

obstetrician, an ear, nose and throat guy, a medical office manager, a woman from a laboratory that made fake skin, and a maxillo-facial surgeon.

Allison was seated next to the surgeon from Chicago, a distinguished-looking older gentleman, and she was fascinated by the stories he told her about reconstructing an accident victim's jaw and replacing a hockey player's teeth.

"I'm doing a tricky surgery next week," the surgeon, Dr. Handel, said. "You'd be most welcome to come and observe. I know of a charming hotel very near the hospital where you could stay." He waggled his eyebrows ever so slightly, and his ulterior motives became clear.

And here she'd thought his interest in her was professional!

Jeff slung his arm around Allison's shoulders. "Some other time, perhaps," he answered for her. "Allison and I have plans for next week. Would you like me to get you a fresh iced tea, sweetheart?" he asked with almost sickly devotion.

Once she got over her shock that Jeff had been listening to her conversation with Dr. Handel, she wondered why he was bothering. Sherry, quite the opportunist, was busy flirting with the obstetrician. "No, I think I'll drink water today," she answered just as sweetly.

"Did you enjoy your morning?" he asked, playing with a bit of her hair, tickling her ear with it.

Allison's nerves vibrated from her toes to her

scalp. She had to keep reminding herself that all this affection was counterfeit.

Before she could answer, he spoke again, addressing the surgeon. "I don't mean to divert Allison's attention from you. It's just that we're...well, we're newly engaged."

Dr. Handel, apparently a good sport, smiled widely. "Well, then, let me offer my congratulations. May I kiss the bride?"

Oh, great! Thanks a lot, Jeff.

"I'm afraid that's a privilege I reserve for myself," Jeff said smoothly just before he swooped in and kissed her full on the lips. It wasn't a gentle, teasing kiss, either. It was a full-blown, grinding, lip-locked kiss—a French kiss, she and her friends used to call it in high school. And it affected her like no other kiss ever had. All those previously awakened nerve endings crashed together in a crescendo of desire that heated her core to the boiling point in record time.

Uncomfortable with the public display, Allison gently pushed him away. "What are you doing?" she asked. Her tone was teasing, but the way she stared at him was intended to let him know she was slightly alarmed by his behavior.

"Just making it clear you belong to me," he said easily, though his breathing was uneven. Was it possible the kiss affected him, too?

The others at the table had stopped their conversation to stare with amusement, though Sherry looked more intrigued than amused. Had she guessed there was something not quite right about the relationship between her quarry and his ersatz fiancée? Was she still looking for some chink in the armor of love and devotion?

Allison didn't think she could continue sitting at this table as if nothing had happened, but neither did she want to cause a scene or leave room for too much speculation. She looked at Jeff. "I don't really want to hear the lunch speaker."

"Me, neither."

In unison they put their napkins on the table and slid their chairs out. Allison kept a wary eye on Jeff, in case he decided to make another unpredictable move. But all he did was meet her gaze, rather boldly, she thought.

"Y'all are leaving?" Sherry asked. "But you'll miss dessert. They're serving raspberry fudge cake."

"I think they've got their own dessert in mind," the obstetrician said in a stage whisper.

Allison wanted to object. That wasn't the impression she'd meant to leave. But to argue the point would just draw attention to it. She picked up her purse and tote bag. "Nice to meet all of you."

Sherry gave her a forlorn little smile as Allison whisked herself away from the table, nearly knocking down a waiter with a tray full of raspberry fudge cake. If she'd thought she could get away with it, she'd have nabbed a slice from the tray and taken it up to her room.

Jeff was following right behind her as she wove her way out of the crowded ballroom. He caught up to her as she made her way through the lobby toward the elevators.

"What was *that* all about?" he demanded.

The question was so unexpected Allison skidded to a stop. "You're asking *me?* You're the one who gave me an unsolicited tonsillectomy back there in front of five thousand people." She resumed walking.

"I had to do something. You were…cuckolding me."

"No, Jeff, I've got news for you. He was flirting with me. I was not flirting back."

"Well, I couldn't just let him get away with it."

"Why not, for heaven's sake? No one else was even paying attention, and it wasn't as if he was going to compromise my virtue. I'd have turned him down on my own."

"You sure about that?"

Allison stopped in front of the elevator bank and savagely punched the up button. "He was old enough to be my father!"

"You certainly seemed cozy with him."

She'd had enough. The elevator door opened onto an empty car, and Allison stepped inside. "That's it. This fake engagement is over."

"Come on, Allie," he cajoled as he followed her and pushed the button for their floor.

"No, I mean it. I was happy to run interference for you with Sherry. I didn't mind walking around the hotel on your arm. But your kissing me in pub-lic—I mean, not just a friendly peck on the cheek, but kissing me like you wanted to ravish me right there on the table—that's taking this play-acting a little too far.''

Jeff was quiet, too quiet.

''Well?''

''Maybe I wasn't play-acting.''

Now it was Allison who couldn't find any words. Was she hearing things? Had Jeff just said—but surely he couldn't mean what she thought…

But the way he was looking at her said he meant exactly that. He took a step toward her, then another, and suddenly Allison didn't want to fight anymore. She melted into him as he put his arms around her, and she turned her face up to his, no longer alarmed by the thought of his kissing her.

Finally the moment she'd been waiting for her whole life was about to happen.

Chapter Four

Jeff's anger abruptly fled, replaced by a yearning so strong it actually made him light-headed. Before he could stop himself, he had Allison in his arms, and she was looking up at him with an expression as sweet and open as a daisy.

There was no decision on his part. He moved into the kiss as naturally as breathing. The softness of her lips against his felt as new and exciting as if it was the first kiss he'd ever experienced, as if maybe all those other girls and women he'd kissed during his lifetime had been merely dress rehearsals.

The elevator came to a halt and the doors opened on the fifteenth floor. Moving through a soft haze of desire, Jeff took Allison's hand and led her down the hall. They exchanged not a word, as if they were of one mind and communication was unnecessary.

At least, he hoped that was the case as he fumbled to get the magnetic card into the lock. He hoped she was thinking the same thing he was—that they would make a beeline for that luscious king-size bed and make passionate love for the rest of the afternoon.

He finally got the door unlocked and held it open for Allison. She walked past him, her brown eyes dreamy, her movements slow and deliberate. She dropped her purse and tote bag on the ground just inside the door, then stopped and waited for him.

She didn't have to wait long. Whatever the spell was that had come over them, he didn't want to break it. She gave a small squeal of surprise as he whisked her into his arms. The bedroom door was ajar, and he kicked it the rest of the way open and carried her in and onto the bed.

It would have been easy to just go with the momentum, strip off his clothes, strip off *her* clothes if she didn't beat him to it, and slake his desire in a white-hot blaze of whirlwind sex. But this was Allison. She wasn't some one-night-stand tart who merely had an itch that needed scratching. She was his friend, someone who lived in his hometown, a professional associate, with connections to his family.

She was a minister's daughter, for pity's sake.

While he stood momentarily frozen with indecision as to how to proceed, Allison sat up, then slowly worked the zipper down the front of her little red dress, her gaze on him. As the shadow between her breasts came into view, his mouth literally watered.

How could it have taken him so long to notice what a fantastic body she had?

"You gonna lose those clothes?" she asked, her voice quavering.

To hell with caution. Jeff nearly sprained his fingers unbuttoning his shirt and peeling it off. He unfastened his belt, but he was too distracted to do much more as Allison stood and the red dress dropped to the floor. A wisp of red lace barely covered the tips of her generous breasts, and the matching panties—

"Have you been shopping at Hollywood Lingerie?" he asked in a hoarse voice.

"You bet."

He'd been in there once, when his nurse, Molly, had been helping him buy a gift for a lady friend. He'd almost died of embarrassment, and he wasn't that easy to embarrass. It was nearly impossible for him to imagine conservative, staid Allison shopping there.

Impatiently she reached for his belt buckle and finished the job he'd started. What was wrong with him, standing there like a tree trunk when a gorgeous woman in barely there red silk underwear was trying to undress him?

He moved back into action, shucking his pants, shoes and socks in record time. Almost before he'd kicked the discarded clothing aside, Allison pulled him down to the bed with her. Though they were both still in underwear, Jeff couldn't remember ever feeling so exposed, so naked. Every inch of his skin was aware of the female form next to his. Her skin was hot to the touch, her hands like miniature electric blankets as they grazed his arms, chest, back, legs.

Allison had somehow taken the lead in this encounter, and that was something Jeff wasn't accustomed to. He liked to be in control, to orchestrate who did what and when. Allison's unexpected initiative left him feeling unbalanced—and unbelievably excited.

He pressed her back against the mattress and kissed her again, more urgently this time, invading her with his tongue, tasting her, drowning in the scent of her skin, her hair. He didn't think she was wearing perfume, not since he'd told her to take it off last night, but she didn't have to. Her own special scent was familiar to him in a new way. He must have encountered it many times before, but he'd never been aware of it until now. Suddenly it was a powerful aphrodisiac.

While still exploring her mouth, he unhooked the front clasp of her bra and let her breasts spill into his hands. He couldn't believe what was happening—he was touching Allison's breasts. It seemed as if maybe he'd dreamed this before, perhaps many times. But such dreams, if he'd really had them, must have been brutally repressed.

Allison, forbidden Allison, his friend, his buddy, his convenient, nonsexual escort, taken for granted all these years. Had he been completely blind, and stupid, too?

Though she made a great show of eagerness, Allison's actions did not seem to be those of a practiced seductress. It occurred to him that she probably was not very experienced, despite her maturity in other respects. He also knew that his lovemaking was, as a rule, very intense, or so he'd been told by other women.

He hoped he didn't overwhelm her, but he doubted he could hold back. His passion was more like possession. Once it took him over, he was a prisoner of it. He'd had no complaints in the past, but there was always a first time.

ALLISON, who by now had touched him everywhere on his body but the place where it really, really counted, screwed up her courage and dipped her hand into Jeff's boxer shorts, clasping her hand around him. She was rewarded with a sharp intake of breath and an even sharper one when she started to move her hand in a caress.

Now what?

She was not completely without sexual experience. In college she'd become determined to dispense with her awkward virginity, and the target of her seduction had been about as sensitive as a pile driver. She'd had other, better experiences, some of them downright pleasant. But she'd always been the slightly reticent, passive participant. She'd certainly never launched her own sexual foray.

"Allison," Jeff said on a gasp, grabbing her wrist.

She'd done something wrong?

"A little too much, um, stimulation. Unless you want this to end sooner than expected."

"Oh." She stopped her somewhat frantic seduction attempts, and instead focused on freeing Jeff from his soft knit boxers. The room wasn't bright, since they hadn't turned on a light, but some daylight filtered through the partially opened curtains. Allison spent a few moments just admiring Jeff's body.

Better, much better than her fantasies.

Jeff followed her lead, divesting her of her panties and bra.

They were naked. Together. She pressed her body against his and thought that if she died right now, she would have achieved her fondest wish. Even the actual act of making love was secondary to the pleasure of lying naked in Jeff's arms and the sweet ache of anticipation. She was aware of every point of contact, the rough feel of the hair on his legs, the firm, possessive grasp of his hand on her hip.

As casually as possible, Allison reached for the bedside table and retrieved a foil package she'd planted there, even though at the time she'd thought it was hopeless. She thought Jeff must be ready to culminate this amazing event.

But he wasn't quite done with his foreplay. He kissed her breasts, making her writhe with pleasure. A flame burst to life in the pit of her belly and a strange trembling invaded her limbs, momentarily paralyzing her.

An innocent brush of his fingertips along her hip made her gasp; the less innocent tip of his tongue in her navel made her cry out.

Why, in a million years, had she thought the actual act of making love was somehow secondary? Suddenly it became the most important thing in the world to have Jeff inside her, filling her, completing her.

Ready now for him to hurry along, she reached for his erection again, stroking him, coaxing him. The foil packet was still clutched in her hand. She ripped it open with her teeth. Ignoring her trepidation over her lack of skill in this area, she managed to sheath him without mishap, somehow making the action blend seamlessly into the ocean of caresses and strokes and sighs they were drowning in.

Jeff moved on top of her, resting in the cradle of her thighs for a moment as he gently tested his weight on her. She spread her legs and urged him to enter, expecting a quick, merciless thrust.

But he surprised her again by entering her in slow degrees, until she thought she might explode with the need for completion. Certainly nothing in her experience had prepared her for the sensations now rocketing through her body. She heard a moaning and realized it was coming from her throat, an animal-like sound that was completely unfamiliar.

Jeff plunged deeper now, again and again, his movements ferocious yet in no way hurtful or rough. She reveled in the fierce grace of their sexual dance, in which there were no missteps, no need for apology, no need for words at all. He knew exactly what her body cried out for and supplied it in spades.

When his body finally clenched with spasms of

ecstasy, Allison let go and joined him, the feeling of oneness the most joyful moment of her life.

A few moments later they still lay together, literally panting, their bodies damp from exertion. Little by little Allison became aware of the bed and the texture of the sheets beneath her body, the hum of the air conditioner, the play of light coming through the gap in the curtains and illuminating a strip of wallpaper.

In fact, she noticed everything, her senses overloaded. She was sure she'd been sleepwalking through her life until now, unaware of anything but the most gross stimuli.

Jeff pulled himself away from her and moved to lie beside her, his arms still around her. She was suddenly cold. He sensed this, without her saying a word, and pulled the blanket over them.

One of them had to say something, but words seemed so inadequate. Still, she made a stab at it. "Was that especially good, or have I just been deprived my whole life?"

Jeff chuckled, and Allison relaxed slightly. A dash of humor had been the right approach. Better than any dramatic declarations of undying love, to be met with embarrassed silence. Wanton sex was a long way from love, but at least it was a step in the right direction.

"It was good," he assured her, snuggling closer, absently stroking the side of her breast. "I never imagined…"

But I did, she added silently. Obviously, he'd

never fantasized about her, and their sudden burst of desire had come as a complete surprise to him. She hoped this experience would prompt a change in his thought patterns.

He traced a design over her nipple, causing a new warmth to spread through her chest and down.

"Careful, Jeff, or you'll get me all hot and bothered again."

"And would that be such a bad thing?" His caresses grew bolder as he gently kneaded her breast.

"Only if you don't plan to carry through."

"Ha! Ye of little faith." And sure enough, she did feel something stir against her thigh. Could they possibly? So soon? Maybe they could stay in bed the whole weekend and blow off the rest of the convention.

Gradually Allison realized Jeff's massage of her breast had changed subtly.

"Allison..."

The lovely heat inside her turned to ice water.

"Not to ruin the mood," he continued, "but...I feel something in your breast."

Allison grasped his hand and pushed it away with a sigh. "Yes, I know it's there." She hardly ever forgot about it, in fact, although she'd managed to blot it out of her mind while she was making love.

"Have you had it checked out?"

"Yes, of course." Or she would, this afternoon at her doctor's appointment. "It's nothing."

"You haven't been in to see Dad lately."

"Jeff, give it a rest, okay? You're not allowed to

put on your doctor hat while you're in bed with me. The lump is nothing, just a little fibroid.''

She hated lying to Jeff, but neither did she want to worry him needlessly. His mother had died of breast cancer when he was in high school. She remembered how hard Leanne Hardison's death had hit all of her sons, but Jeff had seemed particularly devastated. He'd been right at the brink of manhood, a time when he'd thought it wasn't cool to show his emotions. For a few months he'd been closed off even to her, his normally sunny personality eclipsed by his grief.

Eventually he'd come out of it, but she was sure he would never forget losing his mother to a slow, painful cancer. Allison refused to bring those memories alive for Jeff, not when her little lump was probably nothing.

"I can't help it," he said. "Being a doctor isn't something I can turn on or off."

She understood that. Like she couldn't help evaluating the teeth of every single person she met. In fact, that was how she remembered people. Dr. Handel had a small chip on his left front incisor she could fix up in no time.

"Anyway, I was just concerned. You wouldn't believe how many women ignore something like that."

"I'm not one of them." She kissed him on his cheek, grateful for his concern. But she'd caught sight of the digital clock near the bed, and if she didn't get a move on, she would be late for her doctor's appointment. Reluctantly she sat up. "Mind if I shower first?"

"You're getting up? I thought we were going to…" He ran one finger down her arm from shoulder to hand, causing all kinds of pleasurable chills. It would be so tempting to forget about the doctor, forget about her lump and indulge herself. She might never get another chance. But then she would be one of those women Jeff had talked about, the ones who ignore potentially serious health problems.

"I have a meeting this afternoon," she said glibly as she dragged herself out of bed, snatching a silk robe from her suitcase and covering herself. Even in her new, slim body, she wasn't comfortable parading around naked.

"Who are you meeting with?" Jeff wanted to know.

"Oh, nobody important," she said with a flippancy she didn't feel. But this was a subject she wanted to drop—fast. She grabbed some clean clothes and slipped into the bathroom before Jeff could pursue it further, figuring he would forget about it before she finished her shower.

JEFF STAYED IN BED, waiting for Allison to finish her shower and trying to come to terms with what had just happened. He'd gone to bed with Allison. He'd had sex with Allison. Allison Crane, his best friend, who had never registered on his sexual radar until yesterday, had turned out to be a sex kitten.

How had he overlooked her for so long? More to the point, what was he going to do now that he'd discovered what he'd been missing?

The answer to that question was painful, but inescapable. He would do nothing. Making love to Allison had been an impulsive act, one he wouldn't have done if he'd had a chance to think about it. Allison was a great girl, but she wasn't his type. The women he dated were usually… *Well, let's face it. They're bimbos.*

He kept company with flashy women who were impressed by his fast car and the M.D. after his name. They liked to have a good time, they didn't ask too many questions, and they didn't expect a lifetime commitment. Most important, they all knew he wouldn't stick around for long. He always made it clear up front that he wasn't looking for a long-term relationship, and he'd never had a problem just walking away when things started getting dull.

Allison was the antithesis of those women. She was way too intelligent, way too analytical, a bottomless well of complex emotions. He couldn't imagine her entering any relationship without believing it could lead to love, marriage, children—all the things he'd managed to avoid his whole life.

A romantic relationship with Allison would not be a simple thing. She would throw herself into it full throttle, the way she did everything, and before long he would feel trapped, smothered, mired in sticky emotional issues. He would end up hurting

her, and his whole family—no, the whole *town*—
would turn on him.

The more he thought about it, the more he realized
giving in to his base impulses had been a huge mistake. Allison deserved better than him. She needed
a constant, down-home kind of guy, a salt-of-the-
earth farmer type who would be a good father to her
children, someone who would enjoy family vaca-
tions to Disneyworld. She didn't need Jeff Hardison.
She'd said it herself—he couldn't commit to a banana.

So how to undo this disaster in judgment with a
minimum of pain? How could he reject her as a
lover and keep her as a friend? He didn't want to
hurt her, but a little pain now would prevent a lot
later. That's what he told kids when he gave them
vaccinations.

He wished he could give himself an anti-Allison
vaccination, so he would never desire her again.

When she emerged from the bathroom, she was
dressed in jeans and a clingy orange shirt. "Hope I
didn't take too long. I tried to hurry."

"No problem." He got up and headed for the
shower, thinking he ought to say something now,
before Allison started building this incident up in her
mind, before she started getting ideas. But she was
completely ignoring him, crawling under the dressing table to plug in her hair dryer—and giving him
a great view of her bottom.

Don't even go there.

As he showered, he rehearsed what he would say to her. About how he valued her friendship, how she was one of his favorite people in the world, how he didn't want to ruin what they had. Everything he came up with sounded lame, clichéd.

"Jeff?" Allison called.

He peeked around the shower curtain. The bathroom door was open a crack, just enough that she could talk to him. "What is it?"

"I have to go. I just wanted to say…well, hell, there are a lot of things to say, and I don't want to yell them at you while you're in the shower. I'll see you later, okay?"

"Okay."

A slight panic gripped Jeff's stomach. It was starting already. She had things to say to him. What sort of things? She wasn't falling in love with him, he hoped.

As he dressed a few minutes later, he felt a little let down that Allison had skipped out on him. He'd sort of wanted to get this thing settled.

He also wanted to know where she'd gone, who she was meeting. Why hadn't she just told him when he'd asked? What could she have to hide from him?

Visions of Allison with Dr. Handel flashed through his mind. No, that was ridiculous. But what if she had a date with someone else? Did she dare go straight from his arms into some other guy's? A woman as hot as Allison was bound to garner interest from other males, as he'd seen at lunch and at the reception last night. Was it far-fetched to believe she was meeting one of them? Maybe Tom?

That would be a good thing, he told himself sternly. The sooner she forgot about him and moved on, the better. Then they could get things back to normal. But he had a sick feeling in his stomach the rest of the afternoon.

"I CAN'T TELL YOU how much I appreciate your squeezing me into your schedule," Allison said to Stephanie Rich, her old roommate. They'd shared an apartment in Dallas while Allison was attending dental school and Stephanie was pursuing her medical degree, which had made them very compatible. No parties, no loud music, no boyfriends cluttering up the place, study all the time. They'd lived on take-out Chinese food and pizza, which hadn't helped with Allison's weight problem, but who had time to cook healthy food?

"It's no problem," Stephanie said as she peeled off her rubber gloves. "I had a cancellation. It was getting you in at the imaging center that took an act of Congress. I'm done, you can get dressed." Ash-blond Stephanie, who never gained a single pound, seemed unusually serious, which didn't put Allison's mind at ease.

"So, what do you think?"

Stephanie smiled. "I can't believe how great you look! Sixty pounds?"

"C'mon, Steph, I wasn't fishing for compliments. You know what I want to know."

Stephanie adopted a more serious expression. "I'll know more as soon as I look at your pictures."

Allison leveled a steady gaze at her friend. "You're holding back."

Stephanie sighed. "It doesn't feel good," was all she would say.

The results of Allison's mammogram arrived just as she finished dressing. Stephanie took the manila envelope from her receptionist and led Allison into her office, where she put the film on a light box and examined it at length.

"You're killing me here," Allison said.

"Okay. My educated guess is, it's a cyst."

"Benign?"

"Yes. But I can't tell for sure. You need more tests."

Allison had relaxed for all of five seconds before she heard more tests. That meant more uncertainty, more waiting, more driving herself crazy.

"I wish I could give you a definitive answer today, but I can't. I want to schedule a biopsy."

Allison's heart rose into her throat. "Surgery?"

"Just a needle aspiration, here in the office. You can go home afterward."

That didn't sound so bad. "Will it hurt?"

Stephanie winked. "You won't feel a thing. Isn't that what you told me when you did my root canal last year?"

"I'm a liar, and so are you."

Despite the banter, Allison was less concerned about the procedure itself than the results. She scheduled the mini-surgery for two weeks. She would be a nervous wreck by then.

Sitting in a cab on her way back to the hotel, Allison forced herself to relax and think about something more pleasant—like her encounter with Jeff. It was strange, the way life worked. She was facing the scariest crisis of her life, yet fate had thrown her something good to go along with the bad. She hated that she'd had to rush off, but maybe she could make it up to him. A romantic dinner in bed? A sensual massage with scented oil? Their suite had a Jacuzzi tub, which sent her imagination soaring.

Not that she could take for granted that Jeff would want to be with her again. But she hadn't imagined his reactions in bed. He'd enjoyed it every bit as much as she had, and she couldn't imagine him not wanting to repeat the experience.

It was late afternoon by the time she reached the haven of her hotel suite. There was no sign of Jeff, for which Allison was both grateful and disappointed. She could use a little decompression time to sort out the events of the day and make plans for the future. But she also couldn't wait to see him again.

Housekeeping had paid them a visit. The bed was made, with a mint on each pillow. Allison absently grabbed one of the mints and started unwrapping it, then stopped herself. She had always turned to food in times of crisis—exactly the sort of behavior that would return her sixty pounds to her. She set the candy aside, pulled off her shoes, and lay down on top of the bedspread. She would just rest for a few minutes.

When next she opened her eyes, it was dark. Alarmed, she switched on a lamp and checked her watch. It was almost eight o'clock. Where was Jeff?

She had a bad feeling about all this.

Chapter Five

Jeff sat in the lobby bar with a couple of sales reps. He'd been sipping on the same watered-down drink all evening, because he'd told himself that as soon as he finished one drink, he would go up to his room, find Allison, and say what needed to be said.

Two hours later, he was still here.

He'd never been in such a predicament before. He'd made the let's-just-be-friends speech at least a half dozen times in his life without much angst. But this was Allison, and everything was different with her.

Still, the longer he put it off, the harder it would be. She was probably wondering where he was. They hadn't made any definite plans for tonight, but it was sort of implied they would stick together.

"Where's that pretty fiancée of yours?" one of the sales reps, a beefy Chicagoan, asked. "You sure keep her on a long leash."

"No, you got that wrong," Jeff replied. "*I'm* the one on a leash. And I guess I better go find her before I get in trouble." Jeff tossed back the last watery drops of his drink, thinking what a liar he was. Allison hadn't acted possessive at all.

"You're not going to dinner with us? You can bring along the lady."

"I think she has plans for us," Jeff replied with a devious smile before taking his leave. And that was exactly the problem. What were Allison's plans for them? More than ever, he wished she hadn't rushed off earlier.

He was relieved when he found her in their suite. She was wearing exercise shorts and a snug T-shirt, sitting on the sofa going through all the brochures and freebies she'd picked up at the trade show earlier. At least she wasn't still with whomever she'd met with this afternoon. He hated to admit it, but he'd been half-afraid she wouldn't return.

She had one bare leg curled under her and the other stretched out along the length of the sofa. At the sight of those long, tanned legs, all Jeff could think about was having them wrapped around him. What was happening to him? He'd seen Allison's legs before, and they hadn't triggered sexual fantasies.

She looked up, her expression wary. "Hi." She moved her leg, making room for him to sit down.

"Hi, yourself. How'd your meeting go?" He sat on the opposite end of the couch from her. One of the advertising cards she'd picked up was attached to a bag of Hershey Kisses. Jeff unwrapped one and popped it in his mouth.

"I've had better meetings."

He found himself cheered by that news, then immediately berated himself. Things would be much simpler if Allison found herself a boyfriend.

"Any, um, plans for the evening?" he asked.

"To tell you the truth, I'm exhausted. I thought I might order a pizza and a movie. Don't look at me like that. I worked out this morning, so I can eat pizza."

That was Allison's rule. If she rode her bike, she could pig out. If she skipped her workout, she was limited to rabbit food and yogurt. But the look he'd given her had been unrelated to her dietary choices. He'd been thinking about how cozy her plans for the evening sounded, and whether he was invited.

At least if they stayed in, it would give him plenty of opportunity to make the speech he had planned.

"Am I invited?" he asked casually.

"Do you...want to join me? I mean, if you've got something else you need to do..."

"No, I'm free."

He unlaced his shoes and kicked them off. There were all kinds of things he could do tonight. This was party night at various corporate suites. He could fill up on stuffed mushrooms and cheese cubes and free, cheap wine while letting the sales representatives convince him their companies sold the best cotton swabs or whatever. But the idea of spending a quiet evening with Allison held much more appeal.

And why shouldn't it? He'd always enjoyed spending time with Allison. He remembered long, unstructured summer days from childhood when they would get together in the morning, ride horses, eat a picnic lunch, spend the afternoon at the swimming hole, then climb up to the loft in the old barn and read—Allison with her Nancy Drews and him with James Bond books he'd smuggled out of his grandfather's collection. They'd never seemed to get tired of each other.

Just because they'd gone to bed didn't mean that had to change. All he had to do was convince her they'd made a mistake, and everything would be all right. The awkwardness between them would dissipate.

"What movie?" he asked.

"Something mindless."

"What pizza?"

"Sausage and mushroom, what else?"

"Okay, you're on. I'll handle the pizza, you can pick the movie."

ALLISON'S HANDS SHOOK as she pushed the buttons on the remote control that would eventually deliver the latest over-the-top action movie. Was Jeff just going to pretend this afternoon had never happened?

He certainly hadn't gone out of his way to show her any affection.

The creepy premonition she'd had when she'd awakened in the empty suite a few minutes ago returned with a vengeance. Jeff was acting weird—or rather, he was acting so normal that it was weird under the circumstances—and she was pretty sure she knew why. He was regretting their impulsive actions, and now he was in denial.

She heard him talking on the phone in the bedroom, ordering a deep-dish pizza from some local emporium, along with the appropriate soft drinks. He didn't even need to ask her what she wanted—he knew her that well. It made perfect sense to her that two people who knew each other as well as she and Jeff, and who were obviously sexually compatible, were meant to be together.

Unfortunately, she suspected Jeff felt differently, and that suspicion was slowly chipping away at the edges of her rosy dreams for a romantic evening, not to mention the castles in the sky she'd been building pertaining to the more distant future.

When he rejoined her in the living room, he'd changed into sweatpants and a University of Texas T-shirt.

"Oh, how dare you wear that piece of trash in front of me?" She nodded toward the shirt. "You know it gets me riled." Allison had done her undergraduate work at Texas A&M, and the two schools were staunch rivals.

"That's why I wore it," he shot back. "Got to keep you Aggies in your place."

It was old, familiar banter, somehow out of place given their new and unfamiliar relationship. Well, Allison wasn't going to let him get away with it.

She looked him right in the eye as he settled back on the couch and picked up the remote control. "Are we going to talk about what we did this afternoon, or would you rather pretend it never happened?''

Jeff, momentarily frozen by her unexpected salvo, put the remote back down. ''I think we should talk, by all means. I was just waiting for the right time.''

Knowing Jeff, that time would never happen. She loved him dearly, but he was one of the world's worst when it came to talking about anything personal.

''No time like the present.'' Allison wanted to get this over with. ''It took me by surprise. How about you?''

''To put it mildly.''

''We maybe should have thought it through before we behaved so impulsively.''

''We did let our hormones run amok.''

The conversation ground to a halt. Allison picked at a loose thread on her shorts. Jeff repositioned the pillow behind his back.

''Okay, here it is,'' Jeff said, a new determination in his voice. ''I'm very fond of you, Allie. You're my best friend, and I would never intentionally hurt you. But I feel like my actions today were less than respectful of your feelings. I was careless, and you're too special of a person for me to trifle with.''

Trifle with? He'd thought making love, the most mind-blowing experience of her life, was trifling?

''Our friendship is too good,'' he went on relentlessly, ''and I'm afraid we'll muck it all up if we add sex into the equation.''

Funny, she'd thought sex would enhance their friendship. How wrong could she have been?

Jeff gave up on the pillow, tossed it aside, then stood and began pacing. "You're the one who said I'm commitmentphobic, and I don't deny it. But I've always believed you were the kind of woman who wanted, who *deserved,* commitment."

Allison thought she was going to hurl. This speech sounded so well rehearsed, it could have come out of a can.

"Maybe that's why I never crossed a certain line with you before, in all the years we've known each other."

She wanted to scream. She'd been prepared to let him off the hook gracefully, but not when he was shoveling all this malarkey at her.

"I never heard so much bull," she said baldly, causing him to snap his mouth shut before he could utter whatever ridiculous thing he'd been about to say. "You never crossed a certain line with me because I was fat."

"What?"

"You heard me."

"But…you're not fat."

"Duh! That's because I lost sixty pounds. I don't consider it a coincidence that you didn't 'cross the line,' as you put it, until I'd made myself into an acceptably attractive partner for you."

"Sixty? Sixty *pounds?*"

"I'm not blaming you. I'd just prefer you to be honest about why you suddenly felt compelled to jump in bed with me."

JEFF WAS STILL STUCK on the sixty pounds. He'd never really considered Allison's weight. She'd always seemed sort of shapeless to him, so he'd never thought much about what was under the loose clothes she wore. On some level he must have known that all that bike riding she did had improved her body. But when he suddenly found himself attracted to her physically, he just figured he'd never paid attention to her physical attributes before.

"Maybe," he said when he found his voice, "maybe I never jumped into bed with you because you never flirted with me before. You're right, I did notice a change in you. But it had more to do with the way you were acting, rather than what was on your bathroom scale."

She didn't deny it. Now that Jeff thought about it, she'd been behaving a bit strangely this whole trip— the revealing clothes, high heels, perfume. All of those things, while he hadn't consciously registered them, had been working on his subconscious.

Had she purposely set out to seduce him? The possibility was a bit alarming, and undeniably exciting.

Finally she responded. "I was beginning to think you were blind, you know. It wasn't just losing weight. I changed my hair, my clothes. I started wearing makeup. But you didn't seem to notice. At least, not till today."

How could he have not noticed? "I just thought you'd always been a knockout and I'd been too stupid to realize it."

She blushed and went to work on that loose thread again.

"The issue isn't your desirability—which you have plenty of. It's that I don't think you want to start anything with me."

There was a long pause. Allison brought her knees up to her chin, crossed her arms over them and rested her chin there, as if trying to work something out.

At least she hadn't started crying. One thing he couldn't handle was a woman's tears. Come to think of it, though, he hadn't seen Allison cry since before she could vote.

Jeff perched on the arm of the sofa. Was she ever going to say anything?

Finally she issued a long, soft sigh. "I don't know how to say this except to blurt it out. I think we made a huge mistake, and I'm so relieved you have reservations, too."

What?

"Your friendship means so much to me, and you're so right—throwing sex into the mix might ruin things. Anyway, neither one of us is ready to settle down. I mean, I'm finally gaining a little self-confidence with men. I don't want to tie myself down before I have a chance to have some fun."

This wasn't at all what he'd expected her reaction

to be. But it was good, he told himself. She wasn't hysterical or throwing things at him.

"Anyway, Cottonwood, Texas, just isn't ready for its doctor and its dentist to have a wild fling. We'd be the talk of the town, and you know how bad the gossip can get. All my blue-haired patients would be so scandalized they would start going to Tyler to have their teeth fixed."

She was right about the gossip. Allison's father was the minister at the church attended by the Hardisons. If Reverend Crane learned that Jeff had compromised his daughter, the whole Hardison family might be barred from services.

"So we're agreed?" Allison said. "We'll pretend this afternoon never happened."

"Agreed." That one word was surprisingly hard to say.

She picked up the package of Hershey Kisses and ate the remainder of the candies while they watched The Weather Channel and waited for the pizza to arrive and their movie to start.

ALLISON'S TRAVEL ALARM went off at 5:00 a.m. Last night she'd decided to get up early and get out of the hotel room while Jeff was still asleep. There was an early session he wanted to attend, so she doubted he would squeeze in a workout this morning. But he wouldn't get up at five, either.

If she timed it just right, she could avoid seeing him altogether.

She didn't trust herself around him, she thought

as she pulled on her socks and shoes. Her feelings were still too raw. She was one hell of an actress—she'd done an admirable job last night of pretending she wanted to be just friends, but nothing could be further from the truth.

Still, what was she supposed to do? She wasn't going to humiliate herself by trying to talk Jeff into wanting her. She might not be experienced when it came to love affairs, but she knew something about human nature. A person could not be convinced to feel a certain way about a certain person. She had Jeff's friendship, and she would have to be satisfied with that.

As she tiptoed through the living area toward the door, she couldn't help pausing to take a quick peek at Jeff, sound asleep on the sofa. He was contorted into an impossible position, but apparently the small confines of his makeshift bed hadn't harmed his ability to sleep.

Allison took a deep breath to stop her heart from expanding right through her rib cage. He was so handsome, his face relaxed, content, boyish. She resisted the urge to ruffle his blond hair or tuck his blanket more securely around him.

Your goal is escape, remember? she reminded herself, forcing her feet to march her toward the door.

She worked out at the hotel health club with a vengeance, setting the stationary bike on a program of steep hills, and pedaling until her thighs burned and her clothes were drenched with sweat. She followed the bike with some weights, so her arms would get a workout, too. Then she sat in the sauna for twenty minutes, sweating out the unhealthy effects of high-fat pizza and candy from last night.

Ugh, that candy. But she'd been desperate for some familiar solace.

In the shower she forced herself to examine the lump in her breast, something she'd avoided since first discovering it. It wasn't very big, about the size of a pea, but in breast-cancer terms that was pretty large.

Hard to believe something so tiny could alter one's world so dramatically. She tried to imagine herself making the decision to let some doctor remove her breast, but she couldn't. She liked her breasts. She'd so recently learned to love her body. It didn't seem fair that she might now be forced to do something so destructive to it.

Better than dying, she reminded herself.

As she turned off the water, she cautioned herself not to get carried away. Chances were still very good she did not have cancer. Just not quite as good as they'd been before her visit to the doctor yesterday.

Jeff was gone when she returned to the room, exactly as she'd planned. She put on a jean skirt and a white, ribbed-knit shirt. Before putting on sandals, she painted her toenails with sparkly blue polish, hoping the whimsical detail might brighten her mood.

No one approached her as she walked the tradeshow floor. Even the vendors hardly noticed her. She was the same person she'd been yesterday, when she'd drawn men like ants to a picnic. Today she couldn't even sustain eye contact with anyone.

She supposed her dark mood colored everything. She imagined it like a force field, keeping everyone away from her or worse, making her invisible. A high school counselor had once told her that a winning attitude would make people like her, and that her weight had little to do with her lack of dates. She'd always thought that was a bunch of baloney. But maybe the counselor had been right.

"Allison?"

Allison's heart gave a happy little skip at the sound of Jeff's voice. Even though she'd wanted to avoid him, she couldn't help her Pavlovian reaction to him. She'd loved him so long, and her need to be with him tried to override her common sense.

She smiled, finding she didn't even have to force it. "How was your workshop?"

He rolled his eyes. "Boring. Ready for lunch?"

Allison realized she was starving. Somehow, she'd managed to skip breakfast, which surprised her. She never skipped meals. Some people lost their appetite when they got upset. Not Allison. At least, not until today. The fact she hadn't even noticed her empty stomach until now worried her.

"I'm ready." She thought about warning him not to French-kiss her again at the lunch table, then decided against it. She suspected he already knew better than to repeat his performance of yesterday.

Jeff stopped suddenly. "Oh, wait, I forgot. There's just one more booth I want to visit."

"Okay."

The two of them walked along, Jeff leading the way, a map of the convention floor in hand. He turned down a side aisle, walked halfway down, then stopped in front of a display of naked women.

Allison was startled, until she realized the women were mannequins, and they were naked because they were displaying prosthetic breasts. The vendor was Alpha Mastectomy Services.

A horrible feeling overcame Allison. She'd tried really hard not to think about her stupid lump, about the tests she would have to undergo in two weeks and the possible results, but this booth suddenly made it all very real—and frightening.

Her throat started to close. Her face felt hot, and her eyes filled with moisture. Only one instinct prevailed—escape.

"Excuse me," she choked out before making a beeline for the exit.

The speed walking had a calming effect. Just getting away from those mannequins helped. If she could get a drink of water, maybe a breath of fresh air, she would be all right.

She found herself in the middle of the lobby with no idea which way to turn. She stood immobilized, tears again forming, feeling paralyzed.

Footsteps approached from behind. "Allison, honey, are you all right?"

Oh, God, not Sherry. But it was her, all right,

staring into Allison's face, her forehead furrowed with concern.

"You're crying!" Sherry announced.

"I'm okay," Allison managed. "Just...an allergy attack."

"Oh, bull hockey, I'm a nurse. You think I don't know what an allergy attack looks like?" As she spoke, she led Allison to a sheltered alcove and sat her down on a sofa. "Now you better tell me what's wrong. It's not me, is it?"

Allison almost laughed. "No, Sherry, it's not you."

"'Cause, believe me, I might be flirting with Jeff, but he's not flirting back. He's as devoted to you as a tick to a hunting dog."

Now Allison did laugh. "That's nice to know." Even if it wasn't anywhere near true. "It's nothing, really. I'm okay."

"You're not. You're hurting, I can tell. I can't stand to see people hurting. That's why I became a nurse."

Allison couldn't believe it, but suddenly she had an urge to confide her problem to Sherry. She had told no one, not even her mother, not even Anne. And Sherry *was* a nurse, a health professional.

"Did you and Jeff have a fight?" Sherry asked gently.

"No. I just...I found out yesterday I might have breast cancer."

To her credit, Sherry didn't gasp or look horrified. She just put her arms around Allison and hugged her. "I know how frightening that can be. I went through something similar a few years ago, though it turned out to be nothing."

"Really?" For the first time Allison considered Sherry as a real person, not an enemy or a rival or even a tactical problem. She was a woman with a history, a family, relationships, a whole bunch of factors that had made her into the person she was today.

"I had to have a biopsy."

"I'm doing that needle thing in a couple of weeks."

"It's probably nothing. Most of them are, you know. I've seen a ton of cases. There's nothing better than watching a woman's face when her doctor tells her she doesn't have cancer. I bet it'll be the same with you. But I can tell you that till I'm blue in the face, and you're still gonna spend a miserable two weeks."

Allison nodded.

"Is Jeff being supportive? Or is he being a jerk, like most men?"

"I haven't told Jeff."

Sherry looked scandalized. "Why not? If he's planning to marry you, he has to take the bad with the good. If he can't handle adversity, better find out now."

Allison started to come up with an excuse, or a promise that she would tell Jeff that night, but she found the idea of lying to Sherry suddenly distasteful. "He's not my fiancé," she said.

Now Sherry did gasp. "You broke up?"

"We were never engaged."

"Then why…" Sherry stopped, the wheels in her mind turning. Then her face fell. "He was trying to discourage me."

"Not you specifically," Allison hedged. "He said he always parties too much at these conventions. He wanted an excuse to bow out early."

Sherry slumped back on the sofa. "Thank you for trying to spare my feelings. Damn, I'm always doing this."

"What?"

"Scaring men away."

Allison could see how that might be true. Sherry did come on pretty strong. "Some men don't like assertive women," she said carefully.

"I know, but I didn't think Jeff was one of those. He seems very secure. Anyway, he likes you, and you're assertive. Well, you're not some simpering ninny, anyway."

"He doesn't like me. That was just an act."

Sherry shook her head. "Oh, no, honey, trust me. He wants to jump your bones. If he hasn't already." She gave Allison a sideways look. "Has he?"

Allison had to laugh at the other woman's bold curiosity. "That's none of your business."

Sherry laughed, too. "Okay, okay. But if he doesn't want me—and clearly he doesn't—I'd like for you to catch him and turn him into an honest man."

"I don't plan to turn anyone honest until I get this cancer thing settled."

Sherry turned serious. "If you need someone to talk to, you can call me. Since I've been through it." She pulled a business card from her purse. "Call anytime."

Allison examined the card. Sherry was from Plano, a huge suburb north of Dallas. "You're free-lance?"

"Yeah, since I got fired from my last job. I was kind of hoping I'd make a connection here, but so far, no luck. Anyway, I don't want to get into that. Hey, you want to have lunch? Not in the banquet hall. I can't stomach one more rubber-chicken meal. There's a great Italian place around the corner."

Allison suddenly remembered she was famished. "Let's do it." She felt only a small pang of guilt over abandoning Jeff. But now that the jig was up, she certainly didn't have to play the role of his fi-ancée.

Chapter Six

"I swear, those Hardison brothers have heads like rocks," Anne said as she cast her fishing line out into the softly rippling water of Town Lake.

"You can't blame the man just because he refuses to fall in love with me," Allison argued. Her own fishing line was slack, reflecting her lack of interest in the sport. Anne had suggested they borrow her father's bass boat and go out on the lake so they could talk uninterrupted. But they hadn't had a nibble all afternoon, and there was nothing more to talk about.

"Love isn't the problem," Anne insisted. "It's commitment. Wade and I both had a bit of a problem with that, but it didn't mean we weren't in love."

"Jeff isn't in love. Can we talk about something else?" They'd been hashing over the events of the convention for hours. Allison hadn't intended to blab everything, but Anne had a way of worming information out of her, and pretty soon she'd been confessing every grisly detail of her flash-in-the-pan romance with Jeff.

"If you're giving up on Jeff, then you need to move on," Anne said in her oh-so-practical voice.

"To what?"

"There *are* other eligible bachelors in Cottonwood."

"Hah! Name one."

"How about…Jonathan?"

"Hardison? You're kidding."

"He's the right age, stable, good family man, extremely handsome, very unattached—"

"And as hardheaded as they come. No, I don't think so."

"My parents are having a fish fry this Friday night," Anne continued as if she hadn't heard Allison's objection.

"Since when?"

"Since just now. You should call up Jonathan and ask him to take you."

"What? Now, that is ridiculous."

"You know what will happen if you don't?"

"No. What?"

"Jeff will call you Friday morning and say, 'Want to ride with me to the Chatsworths' fish fry?' And you'll say, 'Sure, why not?' Any excuse to be with him, even though you say there's no chance for a relationship."

Allison made no reply, because what Anne had said was, sadly, true. That was exactly what would happen.

"Wouldn't it be so much better if you could say, 'Oh, sorry, Jeff, but I have a date to the fish fry'?"

"You're not suggesting I try to make Jeff jealous, are you? Because that's really juvenile."

"I'm suggesting, Allison, my dear friend, that you get over Jeff and move on. How many years have you wasted on him? You're thirty-five. You should be married with children."

"Oh, just because you're the poster child for domestic bliss—"

"Are you saying you *don't* want to be married and having children?"

Allison thought about Anne and Wade's baby, Olivia, just two months old. Allison had to confess, a yearning deep inside her stirred to life every time she held Olivia. She did want to be a wife and mother, and there was that cruel biological clock to think about.

Allison reeled her line in. Her hook was bare, the bait having been stolen by a turtle, probably. She stuck another piece of raw bacon—she refused to use minnows—on the hook and cast it out into the indifferent lake. "I'm not going to marry just anybody so I can have children."

"I'm not suggesting that. I'm suggesting you get out and circulate, open your mind to other possibilities besides Jeff Hardison!"

Allison inexplicably burst into tears.

Anne gasped, dropped her fishing pole and rushed to put her arms around her friend, almost capsizing the boat in the process. "Oh, Allison, I'm so sorry. I didn't mean to bully you. I know I can be really blunt and pushy, and I'm sorry, really, truly."

Allison gulped in air, wanting to laugh and cry at the same time. "It's not your f-fault," she gasped out between sobs. "It's just that, thinking about children made me think of babies and breast-feeding, and that reminded me that I might have breast cancer."

Anne pulled away and blinked a couple of times in surprise. "What?"

"I'm going next week for more tests. It's probably nothing. Statistically speaking, it's probably not cancer. But until I know for sure, I have no business starting anything with anybody."

"Allison, why didn't you say something? Have you been keeping this a secret from everybody?"

"It's not the sort of thing you announce in the church bulletin. I told my mother. And now you. Oh, and Sherry."

"The man-chasing nurse?"

"She's really very nice. Insecure, that's all, and I can relate."

Anne squeezed Allison again. "You want me to go with you for those tests?"

With some effort Allison pulled herself together. "Nah, it's just a little office procedure. I'll be fine."

"Then you have to let me distract you with fun stuff until then. We'll get massages. And manicures. We'll rent *Braveheart*. Oh, and, tell you what, you don't have to call Jonathan," she added, almost as if it were an afterthought. "I'll set you up."

"No!"

But Anne wouldn't take no for an answer, and

pretty soon Allison had agreed to the setup. "You be sure and tell him it's your idea, not mine," she said as she wound her fishing line in for one final cast.

"Don't worry. I'll make it sound real casual." She sighed. "I guess we better go in and rescue my mother from Olivia."

Allison was ready. She'd decided an hour before she didn't like fishing.

ALLISON'S PHONE RANG that very night, and she almost swallowed her tongue when she found Jonathan Hardison on the other end of the line.

"Anne put me up to this," he said up-front. "Not that I wouldn't want to take you out, anyway," he hastened to add. "But everybody knows I don't date much."

Allison laughed. "Don't tell me. Anne's been bugging you to get out, circulate, stop wasting time."

"That about sums it up."

"I guess she thinks she'll kill two birds with one stone by pairing us up."

"And we'll never hear the end of it from Anne if we don't do it."

He was right about that. "Okay then, let's do it. I mean, if you want to." It wouldn't hurt her reputation any to be seen with another good-looking Hardison brother, especially one everyone had written off as "least likely to marry again."

"Sure. It'll be fun. I'll pick you up around seven. Um…Jeff won't mind, will he?"

Allison wanted to hoot with laughter at that one. Instead she managed a dignified, "No, I think not." She gave Jonathan directions to her house, and they hung up. She felt pretty good about the date, surprisingly good. She couldn't remember the last time she'd gone to a party with someone other than Jeff, or even alone. Usually, if Jeff didn't ask her, she figured he might be there with another date, and that convinced her to stay home.

This was the beginning of her new life, she declared, her Jeff-free life. She would still be his friend, but she was not going to be at his beck and call anymore. Jonathan Hardison was just the beginning. There were some very cute guys in her bicycle club. And the deacon in her father's church had always had a crush on her, even before she'd made herself over. He wasn't cover-boy pretty, but he seemed nice, and she should give him a chance.

She consoled herself with the fact that she wouldn't have time to get very deeply involved with any man before her medical test results came in.

"YOU NEED TO GIVE that ankle complete rest," Jeff said to Mrs. Marsden, one of his favorite geriatric patients. She'd twisted her ankle dancing the polka at the Red Dog Saloon out on Highway 17. "Molly can give you a loaner wheelchair."

"No way," Mrs. Marsden said, patting her pink-tinged hair. "I'll hop down the street before I succumb to a wheelchair."

"A walker, then. It's just temporary."

Mrs. Marsden considered Jeff's compromise. "Well, okay. But only for a few days." She slid her injured foot into a gold lamé house slipper. "Will Bud and I see you at the Chatsworths' fish fry tonight?"

"Oh, wouldn't miss it."

"My granddaughter Willomena will be there," Mrs. Marsden said coyly. "She'll be graduating in December from University of Houston. A biology degree, so the two of you will have a lot to talk about."

Lord save him from college girls and their matchmaking grandmas. "I'm sure I'll enjoy meeting her. But I do have a date," he added, his tone regretful.

Mrs. Marsden winked. "Well, it doesn't hurt to hedge your bets."

As soon as Mrs. Marsden had cleared out, Jeff went to the phone and dialed Allison's office number. "Hey, Allie!" he said cheerfully as soon as she came on the line. Things had been a little weird between them since Dallas, but given the terrible mistake they'd made, a little awkwardness was to be expected. He figured time would put things back to normal, and he'd given her...what, five days? Should be enough.

"Hello, Jeff," she said, her tone friendly. "What's going on?"

"I called to see if you were going to the Chatsworths' fish fry."

"Why, yes, I am."

"Great. I'll pick you up around seven."

Silence. Then, "Um, actually, Jeff, I already have a ride to the party."

"Oh. Well, in that case, can I hitch along?"

Another silence. "I have a date."

Jeff suddenly felt dizzy. Allison, a date? "Really, that's nice. Who with?" he asked with studied disinterest.

"Oh, there's my other line. Have to go, bye." She hung up.

Jeff stood there for a moment, the phone receiver in his hand. Who the hell was she going out with? Some Romeo who'd suddenly noticed Allison had lost weight, that she had incredible legs and eyes a man could drown in and lips that—

He squelched those thoughts, forcing himself to return to the matter at hand. Allison was dating someone. Who? The SOB better watch his step, that was all Jeff could say. If he made one wrong move with Allison, Jeff would be all over the guy like plastic wrap on leftovers.

He had a more immediate problem, however. He'd told Mrs. Marsden he had a date to the fish fry, and if he showed up unattached, she would know he'd been fibbing. Worse, she would sic her granddaughter on him. Was there another woman in town who would go with him to the fish fry and not assume he was smitten?

He got out his Rolodex, finally settling on Tamra Renfro, a woman he'd dated when they were in high school. She'd never married, though she was pretty, smart and pleasant.

"Why, Jeff, I'm so flattered," she said when he asked her. "But I assumed you'd heard."

"Heard what? Are you engaged or something?"

"No, I'm out of the closet!"

Ye gods! He'd *kissed* her. He congratulated her, because he hadn't a clue what else to say, but he wondered if he'd been the one to convince her to give up men.

An hour later he was digging the bottom of the barrel. It seemed every single woman in Cottonwood had plans for Friday night. Tonya Green was an ex-cheerleader who worked at the Dairy Queen and still lived at home. Jeff knew she had a crush on him, because she always put an extra cherry on his hot-fudge sundaes. With a sigh he got out the phone book and looked up the number for Tonya's parents.

JONATHAN HARDISON FELT very strange as he stood on Allison's front porch, ringing the doorbell. He hadn't dated since he'd courted his ex-wife ten years ago. Back then, he'd thought Rita was the answer to his prayers. She'd been raised in New Orleans, but she claimed to love small-town life and wanted nothing more than to settle down, help Jon with the animals and have a couple of kids.

The kids had come pretty swiftly, but the settling down hadn't. Rita had quickly grown tired of the sameness of ranch life and the scarcity of parties, movie megaplexes and Neiman Marcus.

Jon had known long before she'd walked out that she was cheating on him, but he hadn't confronted her, hoping she'd outgrow it or something. They'd had Sam and Kristin by then, and he'd wanted to keep the family together for their sake.

She'd departed with little warning. Left the kids behind, thank God, and only showed them a token interest now, taking them for two weeks in the summer and an occasional holiday.

Jon had felt nothing but relief after she'd gone. Certainly his love for her had withered a long time before, and along with it his capacity for ever falling in love again. He didn't want or need a woman in his life. His children provided all the emotional stimulation he could ever want. The very last thing he would ever do was submit them to a series of pseudomothers while he shopped around, trying to find a permanent replacement for Rita.

Conventional wisdom said that when you fell off a horse, you were supposed to get right back on. But did that old chestnut prevail when the horse was a bucking bronco?

As for taking Allison Crane to the Chatsworths' fish fry, he was doing it strictly as a favor to Anne—and maybe to needle his brother a bit. Jeff dragged Allison everywhere with him, to protect him from having to deal with a real relationship. But he was blind if he couldn't see that Allison had unrequited feelings for him. Everyone else knew it. And it seemed cruel that Jeff kept monopolizing Allison's time, possibly giving her false hope, when he was not serious about her.

An attractive woman in a blue denim miniskirt and clingy top answered the door, smiling.

"I'm here for Allison—" He stopped when he realized the woman *was* Allison. "Oh. You look…different."

"Hi, Jonathan. Yeah, losing sixty pounds makes quite a difference."

"So does changing your makeup and hair and clothes," he said, rather bluntly, he realized, but he didn't think of himself as terribly suave when it came to women. He expected them to take him like he was.

"Okay, you caught me," she said as she grabbed her purse and a jacket from a coatrack by the door. "I did a makeover. Also Anne's fault."

"She's a busy little thing," Jon commented. "Mind you, I'm not critical. You look great."

"Thanks." He opened the passenger door of his truck for her, and she climbed in. "You didn't bring your kids?"

"On a date?" He could just imagine that. Eight-year-old Sam would pepper Allison with nonstop questions about everything from the universe to the kind of underwear she wore, and Kristin, six, would try to get Allison to set a wedding date. Kristin had been angling for her father to remarry since she was old enough to talk.

"I wouldn't mind," Allison said. "You know I adore Sam and Kristin."

"Don't worry, they'll be at the fish fry. They're coming with Granddad."

"Good." Allison fastened her seat belt and settled in for the ride out to the Chatsworths', feeling very strange. She couldn't remember the last real date she'd been on. In college she'd dated a little bit, mostly with guys who thought because she was overweight she would be an easy mark—and they'd been right. She'd had a few sexual experiences, trying to determine what all the fuss was about.

She'd only figured out the answer to that question last week in Dallas.

Still, it could have been worse. There was no pressure to impress anyone. She already knew there was zero potential for romance between herself and Jonathan. Not that he wasn't intriguing. He had that rugged, outdoorsy look that came from years of hard work in the sun, yet his brown eyes were soft and his mouth sensual. He was everything Anne had claimed—handsome, intelligent, stable. But he didn't flip any of Allison's switches, and even if he had, she could sense the man just wasn't in the market for a girlfriend.

They chatted easily about the weather and the ranch and Allison's bicycling. Jon was polite to a fault, and when they got to the Chatsworths', he was attentive, sticking by her side like a cocklebur. Truth be told, she actually enjoyed the attention, not to mention the curious glances she got from every other woman at the party.

Jeff had certainly never gone out of his way to make her feel special. He made it clear he enjoyed spending time with her, and he made her laugh and played handyman around her house, but she had never felt that pleasing her was important to him. About every three years he remembered her birthday, but he usually gave her something incredibly practical or downright silly, like a Swiss Army knife or fuzzy dice for her car's rearview mirror.

Jeff wasn't at the party. Allison felt a certain amount of satisfaction, believing that her turndown had caused him to stay home. But her smugness was shattered at around nine when he finally showed up—with Tonya Green on his arm.

Tonya was twenty-three, and her main goal in life seemed to be to date every cute guy in Cottonwood. She looked as if she was about to burst out of her leather bustier, and if her skirt had been any shorter, Allison would have herded all the children out of the room.

She clung to Jeff's arm as though she'd just won him at the State Fair basketball toss.

"Oh, please," Jonathan murmured.

Allison felt her face heating. She told herself she was embarrassed on Jeff's behalf, but she knew that was only half-true. "I need some fresh air," she said to Jonathan.

Jonathan chuckled. "No kidding. If Tonya had worn any more perfume, we'd all need gas masks."

He led her out the back door to a patio, which was decorated with paper lanterns in the shape of pumpkins. The flagstones were strewn with orange glitter.

"Something to drink?" Jonathan asked.

"A root beer would be nice."

Jon fished one out of a cooler and handed it to her along with a napkin. "Do you want a glass with some ice, or is the can okay?"

"The can's fine." Jeez, he was polite. Was he the exception or the norm? Is this the way normal, mature males acted on a date? She hadn't a clue, and that was embarrassing.

She was about to claim a seat at the picnic table when Anne, with Olivia in a Snugly, grabbed her by the arm. "You don't mind if I borrow your date for a few minutes, do you?" she asked Jonathan.

Jonathan smiled and nodded. Anne dragged Allison out into the backyard, where a waterfall gurgled softly into a deep blue swimming pool.

"So, how's it going?"

"Fine. Jonathan is very nice."

Anne waved away her answer. "I know he's nice. I'm talking about with Jeff. You saw him, didn't you?"

"Oh, yeah."

"And did he see you?"

"Why would he even notice when he's got Bambi Bimbo on his arm?"

"Tonya. You mean you ran away before he could notice who you're with?"

"I mean Jonathan and I came out here for fresh

air. I don't give a flip whether Jeff sees me or not."
Liar, liar, pants on fire.

"But—"

"But nothing. Jonathan is a perfectly nice man,
and I won't stoop to using him in some misguided
scheme to make Jeff jealous. Your machinations are
painfully transparent, and I want you to stop."

Anne deflated a little. "You're not really using
Jonathan, you know. He's in on the plan."

"He told me you strong-armed him into asking
me out."

"No, I mean, he wants to make Jeff jealous, too."

"It wouldn't work," Allison said flatly.

"Try it. I'm going to put on some dance music,
and I want you and Jon to get things started."

"Oh, Anne, you're hopeless." But some small,
immature sliver of Allison's personality thought the
idea was appealing. Maybe she couldn't make Jeff
jealous, but she would like to make it clear to him
that he was no longer the center of her universe.

JEFF KNEW he'd made a mistake the moment he arrived at Tonya's front door. Not that Tonya wasn't
a perfectly nice girl, and very pretty, but she was
waaaaaaay too young for him. All she could talk
about was music and driving to Dallas to go to night
clubs. And when she needed a break from that subject, she talked about clothes and shoes and jewelry
and hair.

Women with nothing important on their minds
had always been appealing to Jeff. No challenge, no

pressure. All he had to do was nod and say, "Mmm, hmm," occasionally. He'd been out with dozens of Tonyas. But tonight it was driving him crazy. He would have given just about anything for a meaningful conversation.

When he arrived at the Chatsworths', the first thing he did was look around surreptitiously for Allison, but he saw no sign of her. He was dying to know who she'd wrangled into a date. Not that she had to force anyone, he reminded himself. The way she was looking lately, she probably had guys lining up outside her front door.

When he didn't see her right away, he couldn't help but wonder where she'd gone. Had she and her date gotten bored and left the party, to…no, he wouldn't think about that. Maybe they'd found a secluded…no, he didn't want to think about that, either.

"So, are we going to eat fish or what?" Tonya asked.

"I'm not sure there's any fish left." They'd gotten a late start because he had to wait for her to finish her shift at Dairy Queen.

"Of course there's fish," said Anne, his sister-in-law, who was apparently playing hostess for her parents. "Your father and mine have been working that barbecue grill all night, trying to pretend they're Cajun cooks. It's quite a sight." She led them out onto the patio, where other latecomers were tucking into paper plates filled with crispy golden fish fillets. Off to the side, his father and Milton Chatsworth presided over a brick barbecue grill, wearing aprons and silly hats. The two men had been college buddies, and whenever they got together, the normally staid pillars of society acted like the frat boys they'd once been.

Several of the party guests were dancing on glitter-strewn flagstones to country music issuing from a boom box. Children, shrieking with laughter, darted in and out among the oblivious dancers, playing a game of tag and making up the rules as they went along.

"Do you think they have any red snapper?" Tonya asked.

"Um, no. I don't believe Town Lake has any snapper, just catfish and bass. Maybe crappie."

Tonya wrinkled her nose. "Well, okay."

That was when Jeff saw Allison. The music had switched to a slow song, and he saw her face over the shoulder of some tall cowboy. They had their arms wrapped around each other, and Allison's eyes were closed as though she was really enjoying herself.

"Jeff? Jeff!"

"Huh? What?" Jeff shook himself from the trance he'd been in.

"I asked if you could get me a beer. Blue Ribbon, if you can find it."

"Uh, sure." As he headed for the coolers that held the beer and soft drinks, Jeff stole another look at the impromptu dance floor. Allison and her cowboy had swiveled around, and shock washed over

Jeff as if he'd clamped his hand around an electric fence.

Allison was dancing with Jonathan.

That's who her big date was? How was that possible? Jonathan never dated and hardly socialized. And just what the hell would Allison see in Jonathan anyway? He was so serious, so...so angry at the world ever since Rita left him. Allison was all lightness and laughter. Her sense of humor was one of the best things about her.

At that moment she whispered something to Jonathan, and he burst into laughter. Jeff was sure he'd never heard Jon laugh like that. The sound sent a ripple of confusion coursing through Jeff's blood.

This wasn't right. Maybe Allison had developed some feminine curves and a new attitude, but did that mean she had to throw herself at any single man who crossed her path?

She was apt to get herself in terrible trouble. And Jeff couldn't possibly allow that to happen. As her best friend, it was his job to rescue her.

Chapter Seven

"They make a nice couple, don't they?" Anne had crept up behind Jeff. She had her new baby, Olivia, nestled in one arm, and she watched the dancing couples with a dreamy look in her eye.

"Who?" Jeff asked, playing dumb.

"Jonathan and Allison. Jon's been alone far too long."

"There's a reason for that," Jeff said dryly. "He's as prickly as a porcupine after you poke a stick into its den."

"Nonsense. He doesn't look so prickly now. Maybe Allison is just the tonic he needs."

Jeff folded his arms. "Don't you know better than to play matchmaker? Just because you and my hard-headed little brother managed to find your slice of paradise doesn't mean the rest of the world is going to do the same."

"Now *that* is some awesomely negative thinking. Anyway, I have nothing to do with the chemistry between those two."

"Chemistry! You've got a wild imagination,

Anne." If Allison had chemistry with anyone, it was with Jeff. Hadn't they proved that last week? Chemistry wasn't that easy to find. She couldn't have it with everybody.

"Jeff!" Tonya's nasal voice sang out. "I need my Blue Ribbon. My throat's about parched."

Jeff looked at Anne. "Do you have any Pabst Blue Ribbon in that cooler?"

"No. Your little honey will have to make do with Lone Star."

Jeff fished out a beer for Tonya and a soft drink for himself. He hardly tasted the fried fish or potato salad, and paid scant attention to his date. His attention was with the dancers. Were Jon and Allison going to dance to every song? Didn't they ever take a break?

"Jeff, you haven't heard a word I've been saying," Tonya admonished. "If you're so fascinated with Allison, why don't you just go cut in?"

He turned his gaze to Tonya, ashamed that his behavior was so transparent. "I'm sorry, Tonya. I just worry about Allison, that's all. She's like…a little sister to me."

"I think she's *old* enough to take care of herself. She's a *big* girl. Anyway, don't you trust your own brother?"

Jeff didn't care for Tonya's catty remarks. He'd thought she was nice, if a bit flaky, but maybe he'd misjudged her. "You're right, she's old," he agreed. "Almost as old as me, and that's ancient in your book, I imagine. But Allison's not big, at least, not anymore. You see any cellulite on those legs?''

Tonya took the paper napkin out of her lap and tossed it on the picnic table. ''If you don't mind, when I'm out on a date with a man, I prefer him not to ogle other women's legs.''

''Sorry.'' He was behaving like a jerk, but he couldn't help himself. ''You've got very nice legs yourself,'' he added sheepishly.

Tonya calmed down a bit. ''Well, at least you noticed,'' she said with a sniff. ''I'm glad to see Allison out with someone besides you. It's tragic, the way she moons over you.''

''You've got that a little cockeyed, Tonya. Allie and I are just friends.''

''*You're* just friends. She's got a crush on you the size of that swimming pool.''

''Where did you get an idea like that?''

''For heaven's sake, Jeff, everybody knows that. I heard she's been trailing after you since high school. Don't tell me you flat-out didn't notice. That's ridiculous. Anyone could see she had eyes only for you.''

''Well, that's obviously not the case now.'' Jeff felt unsettled by Tonya's revelation. Surely it wasn't true. Surely that was just idle gossip from a girl who didn't have a clue what she was talking about, who was just trying to get a reaction out of him. Allison was not now, and never had been, in love with him. Wouldn't he have known it?

Tonya took a gulp of beer. ''She does seem to be

pretty wrapped up in your brother. Like I said, it's nice to see.''

Jeff didn't think so. He couldn't put his finger on it, but the idea of Allison with Jonathan just seemed...wrong, somehow.

ALLISON WAS GETTING a little tired of dancing with Jonathan. She'd welcomed the idea at first, because it had given them something to do with themselves. But every time a slow song came on, and Jon put his arms around her, she felt very awkward, and she guessed he felt the same. They always laughed nervously through the slow songs.

She'd also gotten tired of watching Jeff with his *bimbette du jour*. Tonya was exactly the sort of woman Jeff was known to favor—young, pretty and empty-headed. She didn't understand why he wasted himself on girls like that. She told herself she no longer cared, that she was through worrying about Jeff's social habits. But it still made her slightly queasy every time she and Jon rotated on the dance floor and she saw Tonya leaning close to Jeff and laughing.

Allison turned her attention instead to Anne's father, Milton Chatsworth, who had just finished cleaning the grill. He removed his apron and chef's hat, replacing them with a captain's hat and a windbreaker.

"Who'd like to go for a moonlight cruise?" he announced to anybody listening.

"How about it?" Jonathan asked Allison.

"Sure," she replied, relieved. "I'm ready to get off my feet."

Milton had a pontoon boat in his private boat-house. He had room for at least a dozen passengers, and he had no trouble recruiting them. Allison was pleased to see Anne and Wade among those waiting on the dock for an assist onto the boat. She was not so pleased to see Jeff and Tonya.

Did he have to rub her nose in it?

Granted, he had no idea his hanging all over beautiful women bothered her, as she'd never told him so. Usually she managed to avoid witnessing such distasteful displays.

Anne found a seat next to Allison. "How's it going?" she whispered.

"It's going fine," Allison whispered back blandly.

"Jeff is totally wigged out to see you here with Jon."

"I think Jeff is much too busy with his own date to worry about who I'm with." But Allison couldn't help a little heart flutter at the idea that Jeff might be jealous, at least a little.

It was a beautiful night for a cruise. The air was crisp, the almost-full moon reflected in the still water of Town Lake. The only sounds were the low rumble of the boat's motor, the lapping of waves against the hull, and the occasional, plaintive call of an owl.

"I'm cold," Tonya complained.

"Maybe if you wore a few more clothes," Allison murmured under her breath. But she apparently hadn't been quiet enough. Jonathan leaned down and meowed like a cat in her ear.

"Well, it's true," she whispered to him. "What kind of idiot goes out on the lake at night in October without a jacket?"

"One who's angling for her date to keep her warm," Jon answered. And sure enough, Jeff obligingly put his arm around Tonya's shoulders and rubbed her upper arm. She smiled adoringly at him, then kissed him on the cheek.

"I think I'm going to be sick," Allison whispered.

Jonathan slid his arm around Allison's shoulders. "Two can play at this game."

"You think this is a game?"

Jonathan just chuckled, and Anne joined him, leaving Allison feeling like the odd man out.

Milton steered the boat along the coastline, then into a secluded cove where they disturbed a flock of white herons that took flight. The sight was breathtaking, with the moon reflecting silver on the birds' flapping wings.

Allison couldn't help but look at Jeff. She knew him, knew he would be thrilled by the sight as she was, though he wouldn't admit it.

He caught her gaze, and they shared a moment of silent knowing.

"Eww, it smells like fish here," Tonya said, breaking the spell. The rest of the passengers laughed nervously at her outburst.

The boat headed back to the dock after about twenty minutes. Allison started to stand, but Jonathan pulled her back down. "Stay here a minute," he said.

"Why?" Then she realized he wanted to be alone with her. Oh, hell, had she misjudged the situation? She'd assumed Jonathan was an unwilling participant in this date, that Anne had strong-armed him. Was it possible he was really attracted to her?

"It's nice out here," Jonathan said. "Anyway, I'm tired of people looking at us. In case you hadn't noticed, we're the objects of quite a bit of speculation."

"I guess when two people who hardly ever date go out together, it's enough to make folks curious."

Jeff and Tonya were the last to get out of the boat. As they headed up the dock, Jeff paused and glanced over his shoulder, a curious look on his face. Allison looked away as quickly as possible. There was no reason to feel guilty, she told herself. Jeff had made it clear he wanted no claim on her.

Jon put his arm around her again, and she tensed again. What was going on here, really? She just had so little experience when it came to male-female attraction. She didn't know how to tell whether Jon was merely being polite, or if he really wanted to be close to her. She'd been sure they shared no chemistry, but what if she was wrong?

She had her answer a few moments later.

"Do you mind if I kiss you?" Jonathan asked casually. He could have been asking if she wanted a second helping of potato salad.

"Um..." She sort of did mind. But maybe she

should try it. Maybe she should open her mind to the possibility. Jonathan was really handsome—tall, rugged, muscles on muscles from a lifetime of hard physical work on his ranch. A lot of women would give up their acrylic nails to be in her position.

Finally she nodded, and Jon obligingly leaned down to kiss her.

The kiss was quietly polite, neither arousing nor repulsive. It was merely…pleasant. Though, after the way her body had exploded when Jeff kissed her, she knew *pleasant* wouldn't cut the mustard.

She wasn't worried about Jonathan taking advantage of her. She was more concerned about where his head was, whether he was reading more into this date than she or Anne had intended. The last thing she wanted to do was lead someone on. She'd had enough false hopes herself to know how unpleasant they were.

When Jon broke the kiss, she spoke up, feeling a little panicky. "I'm not sure this is a good idea."

He looked up toward the house, then grinned. "Trust me." And he kissed her again, running his fingers through her hair.

This time she didn't wait for him to break the kiss. She did it herself. "Jonathan Hardison, what's gotten into you?"

"I've been a long time without feminine company, that's all. And you're looking pretty hot tonight."

Was this really Jonathan, Jeff's staid, taciturn older brother? Everybody agreed Jonathan was hopeless, resigned to his divorced status. He wanted nothing to do with women because no one could measure up to the glamorous wife who'd abandoned him.

He certainly wasn't acting true to his reputation.

Jonathan kissed her again, this time pushing her back against the boat's cushioned seat.

Allison pushed right back. "Jonathan! Cut it out!"

"Okay, okay." He held up a hand in a defensive gesture, which was a good thing, because she was seized with the impulse to punch him.

"I'm…I'm not that way," she said, feeling bewildered. "Just because I have on a short skirt doesn't mean I'm cheap."

"No, of course not," Jonathan hastily agreed. "I didn't think that at all. But I did think you wanted men to notice you."

"Notice, yes. I'll confess, I enjoy getting attention from men. I've never had that before. But I guess I—I'm giving out mixed signals or something." Suddenly Allison felt as if she was the one at fault— which was ridiculous. Wasn't it?

"Mixed signals. You mean, you want *certain* men to notice you and others to leave you alone."

Was that true? Had she changed her whole appearance, her whole image, solely to please Jeff? She wanted to think she'd transformed herself to reflect her new self-confidence, that she chose her clothes solely to please herself.

But she feared Jonathan had the truth by the tail.

"I apologize if I misled you, Jon."

Jonathan laughed low in his throat. "You didn't do anything wrong, Allison. Now run along. I'll follow at a respectable distance."

She turned and climbed clumsily out of the boat, then made her way swiftly up the dock and across the yard toward the house. Her sight was clouded by tears of confusion and humiliation. What had happened back there? She felt so clueless, so ignorant. She was thirty-five years old, for heaven's sake, yet she still had no idea what signals she was giving out to which men.

Thank God Jonathan was a gentleman. What if she'd been with someone else, someone who hadn't taken no for an answer?

She brushed by Jeff and Tonya on the patio, trying to look invisible. She heard Jeff call her name, concern in his voice, but he was the last person she wanted to talk to at the moment.

Thankfully, she made it to the bathroom without having to explain anything to anyone, which was a small miracle when she saw her image in the mirror. She had mascara circles under her eyes, making her look like a raccoon, and her mocha lipstick was smeared across her cheek and down her chin. Her hair was a flyaway mess, both from the wind and from Jonathan's fingers.

She didn't have her purse with her, but she was able to make quick repairs to her makeup with a wet tissue. She finger combed her hair into some semblance of order and straightened her clothes. There, much better. She would thank the Chatsworths for inviting her, grab her purse, then grab Jonathan and ask him to take her home. And the next time Anne wanted to set her up with someone, she would give a firm "No."

JONATHAN WAS STILL CHUCKLING to himself as he climbed out of the boat and ambled up the dock. Anne would be proud of him. He'd accomplished his mission of making Jeff jealous, and then some. His brother had never looked at him with quite that much animosity.

Normally he didn't approve of game playing. Lord knew he'd gotten enough of that with Rita, his ex. But Anne could be pretty darn persuasive. And, he thought, let's face it, someone had to give Jeff a kick in the butt. Everybody knew Allison had a case for Jeff, but only Anne had figured out that Jeff had similar feelings for Allison. Only, he wouldn't admit it, not even to himself.

Jon had been doubtful at first, but seeing the way Jeff had stared daggers at him all evening, he'd begun to suspect Anne was right. And judging from the way Jeff was striding across the yard toward him right now, the matter was about to come to a head.

As Jonathan stepped off the dock and onto the grass, Jeff met him. Jon was expecting some sort of verbal assault. Instead, Jeff popped him one right on the mouth.

"Hey!" Jon didn't waste much time nursing his injury, which felt like a fat lip. He put his hands up in a fighting stance, intending to defend himself from the next punch.

He wasn't worried about getting hurt. While Jon had been engaged in good-natured brawls with ranch workers, honing his fighting skills and building muscles with ranch work, Jeff had been attending medical school.

"Just what the hell was that for?" Jon asked, though he was pretty sure he knew.

"What'd you do to Allison?"

"I kissed her. Is there a law against that?" That provoked another punch. Jon blocked it with his shoulder. He'd have a bruise, nothing worse. "Cut it out! You're a doctor, for pity's sake. Don't mess up your hands."

"I'll mess up your face! She was crying. She was all smudged and…and disheveled!"

This was definitely the strangest brawl Jon had ever participated in. "What's it to you?" he said, intentionally provoking his brother.

"She's my friend."

"Hey!" someone shouted from the patio. "There's a fight going on down by the boathouse!"

Oh, terrific. He really didn't want this ridiculous family quarrel to be witnessed by the masses.

"I didn't hurt her," Jon said hastily. "I even asked her permission before I kissed her. I was quite the gentleman."

"And she said yes?" Jeff asked, incredulous.

"What's so weird about that?"

Jeff took another punch, this time aiming for Jon's

gut. He managed to graze Jon's ribs, but he immediately launched another attack, this time knocking Jon off balance, then taking him to the ground.

Once on the ground, Jon had no trouble turning events to his advantage. He outweighed Jeff by twenty pounds. Not that Jeff was a lightweight—he was strong, and he had passion on his side. But he didn't have the advantage of years of baling hay and manhandling calves.

The two men rolled a couple of times, until Jon found a way to end up on top. Rather than press his advantage, he hopped up, thinking the fight was over. But Jeff came at him again, forcing Jon to block another punch.

"You're acting like an imbecile, you know," Jon said. "Why don't you ask Allison what happened?"

"This is between us."

"Because you don't want Allison to know you care?"

By now a few onlookers had gathered. Their father was one of them. Ed Hardison started to step in to break up the fight, but Jon subtly shook his head and winked.

Ed stepped back, trusting Jon not to let things get out of hand.

"You have no business taking advantage of her like that." Jeff almost growled the words.

"All I did was kiss her!"

"You had no right to do that. There are a zillion women in Cottonwood who'd love you to take advantage of them. Why'd you have to go and pick her?''

''Why *not* her? You think she should save herself for someone better? Someone like you, maybe?''

The growing number of observers to the fight let loose with a collective gasp. Jon's accusation slowed Jeff down a second or two, but not for long. Faced with the frightening truth, Jeff's reaction was to just get more angry. He launched another salvo at Jon, and Jon was ready.

ALLISON FOUND Deborah Chatsworth, Anne's mother, in the kitchen. Looking prim and proper as ever in a skirt, silk blouse, hose and heels, she was slicing up a huge pan of brownies. Allison's mouth watered. She'd bicycled that morning. She could eat just one.

Then she remembered her mission.

Deborah looked up and smiled. ''Allison, are you having a good time?''

A little too good. ''Yes, it's a lovely party. But I'm afraid I have to leave. I wanted to thank you for inviting me. You and Milton are such good hosts.''

''Why thank you, dear. Would you like to take a brownie home with you?''

Allison started to accept when she heard some sort of ruckus going on in the living room.

Deborah looked alarmed. ''What in the world is that?''

They both rushed into the living room, where most of the party-goers were pouring out the French doors onto the patio. Anne, however, was standing in the middle of the room, looking around. She homed in on Allison and grabbed her arm.

"There's a fight going on down at the boat-house."

"Good heavens!" Deborah looked like she might swoon.

Anne handed the baby to her mother. "Take care of Olivia for me, will you, Mom?" With that she dragged Allison out the door.

A fight? That was the sort of thing one expected to happen in the parking lot of the Red Dog Saloon, maybe, but not in the backyard of one of Cotton-wood's leading citizens.

A crowd had formed down by the lake. Anne and Allison hurried to join it.

"Who's fighting?" Allison asked.

"I don't know. But we have to stop them."

"Why us?" Allison was sure there were plenty of cool heads among the Chatsworths' guests who could stop a fight, although there were probably a few here who thought Friday night wasn't complete without a good bare-knuckles brawl.

"You've got medical training," Anne said. "We might need you."

"I'm a dentist!" Allison protested. Although she supposed she could help if one of these backyard warriors got his teeth knocked out.

Anne dragged her through the crowd until they could see the combatants. Allison had expected to see a couple of good ol' boys who'd had a few too many longnecks, or maybe some hot-blooded high-school boys whose roughhousing had gotten out of hand.

What she didn't expect to see were the two older Hardison brothers duking it out—and nobody lifting a finger to stop them. Neither of them appeared to be badly injured—yet—though Jonathan's lip was swollen, and the sleeve of Jeff's shirt was torn. They both had grass stains on their clothes.

Jeff took a swing, and Jonathan ducked, then laughed. "You never could fight worth beans," he taunted.

"What in the hell is going on here?" Allison demanded of no one in particular.

Tonya sidled up beside her, looking sullen. "They're fighting over you, stupid."

She was too stunned to react at first. Finally she found her words. "Excuse me?"

"You heard me. The two best-looking, most eligible men in Cottonwood are fighting over you. Enjoy it—I'm sure it doesn't happen that often."

Allison resisted the urge to start her own fight with the catty little tart. Right now she had more urgent matters to concern herself with. Jeff had just taken a flying leap at Jonathan and tackled him to the ground. Allison was sure Jon's face was about to take a pounding, but Jonathan somehow twisted and reversed their positions. His actions were defensive only, Allison realized. Jonathan held Jeff pinned to the ground, making no move to inflict any damage.

However, all amusement had left Jon's face. "That's enough, little brother. You gonna calm down?"

Jeff struggled briefly, then stilled. He held Jonathan's gaze a moment, still challenging. Abruptly all the fight went out of him. He nodded, and Jon let him up.

"Fight's over," Milton Chatsworth said in an effort to defuse the situation. "Deborah has fresh brownies on the patio, and she'll be downright insulted if everybody doesn't eat one." A ripple of laughter went through the guests as they turned and ambled back toward the house.

Milton's arms went around Jonathan and Jeff. "As for you two, better go home and sleep it off. If Pete hears about this, he'll tan your hides, I don't care how old you are."

Pete was the Hardison brothers' crusty grandfather, the original owner of the Hardison Ranch. Although he had just turned eighty-one, he'd recently become engaged to his long-time neighbor, Sally Enderlin. They'd been at the party earlier with Sam and Kristin, Jonathan's children, but they'd already gone home.

Allison gave Jonathan a penetrating stare, but he avoided her gaze. Jeff, too, refused to look at her.

Jonathan walked up to Tonya and took her arm. "Come on, I'll give you a ride home."

"Wait a minute," Allison objected, but Anne shushed her.

"Let it be," Anne whispered, pushing her gently toward Jeff.

Allison suddenly realized everyone else had left. Anne, Wade, Jon and Tonya walked away, too, leaving her alone with Jeff.

"Well," she said, "that was a pretty picture. Two grown men carrying on like schoolyard bullies. And at the Chatsworths' home, of all places."

Jeff just stood there, looking like a little boy in the principal's office, awaiting his punishment.

"Are you going to tell me what happened, or do I have to get it from someone else?"

"Let's walk," he said. And because there was nowhere else to walk but toward the dock, he turned in that direction.

Allison considered walking away, but curiosity was getting the better of her. The Hardison brothers fighting over *her?* It just didn't make sense, and she wanted to get to the bottom of it.

So she caught up with him and walked alongside him, waiting for him to explain.

"What happened with you and Jon?" Jeff asked, his voice quiet. She had never seen him look so serious.

"That's none of your business."

"Did he hurt you?"

"God, Jeff, of course not."

"You were crying."

"Not because he hurt me. He said something that hit an emotional chord, that's all."

"What did he say?"

"None of your business," she said again. "And even if he did hurt me, no one appointed you my guardian. We're friends, Jeff, nothing more, as you so eloquently made clear in Dallas. I'm perfectly capable of taking care of myself, and I don't appreciate your intervention. You've embarrassed your family, you've alienated your date, you've humiliated the Chatsworths. For the next month, everybody's going to be asking me what this was all about. What am I supposed to tell them?"

"How about the truth?"

"Which is…"

He sighed. "Seeing you with other men makes me crazy. Thinking about you making out with Jonathan turned me into a homicidal fool."

"You can't have it both ways, you know," she said pragmatically, all the while her heart beating a wild flamenco rhythm. She leaned against the dock railing and folded her arms. "You can't say, 'Let's just be friends,' then object when I want to date someone else."

"You want to date Jonathan?"

"That is completely beside the point. You've got two choices, bucko. You can choose me—assuming I even want you after this appalling display—or you can let me go."

Chapter Eight

Jeff felt as if some alien being had invaded his body. First he'd attacked his brother, and now he wanted to make some major sort of declaration to Allison, to lay claim to her like some caveman.

Come to think of it, dragging her away to his cave didn't sound like such a bad idea.

She stood there staring at him, expecting him to say *something*. To choose.

"You don't have to look like a deer in the sights of a rifle," she said. "I'm not asking you to marry me. I'm not even asking for undying devotion. Shoot, I'm not sure I even want to go steady with you," she said on a laugh.

"Then what?"

"I can tell you what I don't want. I don't want to be just friends. Maybe we never should have made love. Maybe we shouldn't have crossed that line. But we did, and I can't go backward."

"I know. I feel the same way. But, Allie, I am your friend, and because I care about you, I don't want you to date a guy like me. I wouldn't be good for you.''

"Why not? Anyway," she added wryly, "after tonight, who else in Cottonwood would dare even ask me out?''

"I'm not good boyfriend material. It's that commitment thing.''

"Did I ask for a commitment? Truth is, I'm in no position to make a commitment, either. Does this have to be so complicated? Can't we just…be together? For as long as it works for both of us?''

Jeff should have been jumping for joy. It's what he always wanted in a relationship—no strings attached. When it was over, he walked away, guilt-free, knowing he wasn't breaking any promises.

But this was Allison. "You'd settle for that?''

"It's not settling. It's exactly what I want. It's what I've always wanted.''

"Always?" That reminded Jeff of something he wanted to get cleared up. "I've heard from two different people recently that you've been carrying some sort of torch for me. For a long time, I mean. That's not true, is it?''

She laughed. "Only since seventh grade.''

Jeff felt as if he'd been hit in the head with a sack of cement. "How come I never knew?''

"I took great pains to make sure you never knew. Apparently, I wasn't as good an actress as I thought. Other people figured it out.''

"But why not me? Am I blind and deaf?''

She made a great show of pondering that question. "Ummmm…that would be a yes."

"Allison, why didn't you ever tell me?"

"I did! I asked you to the Christmas dance at the country club, and your eyes bugged out like you were horrified and you turned me down flat."

He stared blankly at her. "You never asked me to any dance."

"I did so. In seventh grade."

"Seventh grade! Allison, for God's sake, in seventh grade I hadn't even discovered girls. I was still interested in digging up worms. Suggesting I attend a country club dance was tantamount to inviting me to hell."

"Oh, never mind the stupid dance. I've never said anything to you in more recent times because I knew you would reject me, and no girl wants to set herself up for that."

"But I wouldn't have—"

"Jeff. I was fat and frumpy, and you had a reputation for dating girls with legs up to their armpits and IQs that matched their bra sizes. I didn't exactly fit the mold. You were my friend, and I didn't want to lose that."

Jeff had to think about that for a moment. How would he have reacted if Allison had come on to him before she'd gotten all glamorous? He wished he could say her looks didn't matter at all. He'd certainly never thought of her as fat and frumpy. He simply hadn't considered her physically, sexually. She was his friend, and that was that.

"Maybe you're right," he finally said. "Maybe I've used the wrong yardstick to choose girlfriends."

"It seems to work for you."

"Maybe it used to. But where's it gotten me? I'm thirty-five years old, not some wild college boy anymore. Maybe it's time for a change. Maybe a relationship with a little more depth wouldn't kill me."

"You won't know till you try. And, Jeff, if it doesn't work out, and you want to walk away, I promise not to make a scene."

"If we bomb as a couple, do you think we could ever be just friends again?"

She looked down. "I don't know. I'd like to think we could. You've been an important part of my life for a long time. But things have changed, perhaps irrevocably."

That thought made him a little sad. But he hadn't lost her yet, he reminded himself. She wanted to be his lover, which opened up a whole new set of possibilities.

What the hell. "So…do you want to go out with me tomorrow night, or what?" He winced. What had happened to his legendary smooth talk?

"Hmm, pretty short notice. I'll have to check my calendar. I might have to wash my hair."

"You're going to torture me now, aren't you. Punish me for the way I acted tonight."

But the way she put her arms around him and kissed him wasn't exactly punishment. Sweet torture, perhaps, because he wanted to ravish her right here and he couldn't. But his house was only ten minutes away.

JONATHAN SAT in the Chatsworths' kitchen with an ice pack on his lip. The other party guests had left pretty quickly after the fight. Tonya had found another ride home—some strapping lad barely out of high school who'd been a football star this time last year and still thought he ruled the world.

Wade was helping his in-laws clean up, while Anne sat at the table with Jon, playing nurse.

"Let me see."

He obligingly took the ice pack away from his mouth.

She studied him critically. "Not too bad. The bleeding's stopped. Are you sure your teeth are okay? I bet Allison would fix them for free."

"My teeth are fine. He didn't hit me that hard. I'm just amazed he hit me at all. Jeff's always been the easygoing brother."

"As opposed to me," Wade said as he pulled another plastic trash bag from a box under the sink.

"Yeah," Jon agreed. "Wade's the one I always expected would take a punch at me."

"I almost did last year."

"I haven't forgotten." Jonathan's daughter, Kristin, had suffered an accident last year, and Jon had mistakenly blamed Wade, causing a family rift that might not have healed had Anne not intervened and made them both see they were acting like asses.

"But Jeff? I never even saw him lose his temper before."

"Looks like we unleashed some pretty raw emotions," Anne said.

"Yeah. If I'd known our little scheme would get so out of hand…" He peered out the window toward the blackness of the lake. "What do you suppose they're doing down there? Maybe someone should check on them."

"Not if they're doing what I think they're doing," Anne said. "Could be very embarrassing."

"Anne, really," her mother scolded. Deborah was scrubbing the brownie pan at the sink. "You should know better than to meddle, both of you."

"But they're so perfect for each other," Anne objected. "Jeff just needed a little nudge."

"But what if he hurts her?" Deborah asked. "Or she hurts him? What if the whole thing ends in disaster? Then they'll blame you two."

"Oh, phooey." Anne dabbed at Jon's mouth with an antiseptic-soaked cotton ball. "In the end it's their choice to be together. Whether it lasts forever remains to be seen, but they'll thank me for getting them together. Otherwise, they both would always have wondered."

"They might thank you, but I doubt Allison will thank me. She thinks I'm some sex-crazed cad."

"Jon, what did you do?" Anne asked, alarmed.

Jon grinned. "Nothing so terrible. But I'm awful rusty. My moves weren't so smooth, if you know what I mean."

A new light gleamed in Anne's eye. "Maybe you ought to brush up on those seduction skills. Let's see, who could we—"

"Oh, no," Jon objected. "Don't you go working any of that matchmaking stuff on me. Rita turned me into a very happily divorced man."

Anne started to object, but the conversation was halted by the sound of the French doors opening. A few seconds later Jeff and Allison entered the kitchen. They weren't holding hands, but Anne could tell just by their body language that they'd reached some sort of understanding.

"Hey, Jon," Jeff said sheepishly. "How's the lip?"

"Swollen, thanks to you. You're crazy, you know that? I could have flattened you."

"I know." Allison jabbed an elbow into Jeff's ribs, prompting him to continue. "Deborah, I'm really sorry I ruined your party."

"You didn't ruin it," she said dryly. "It was the liveliest party we've had in years."

He looked at Jon. "Did Tonya get home all right?"

"She hitched a ride with Ralph Plotsin. They made a very attractive couple."

Jeff didn't appear bothered in the least. "In that case, do you mind if I appropriate your date?"

Jon narrowed his eyes at his brother. "You do right by her, or next time I *will* flatten you."

"Yes, sir."

ALLISON FIDGETED in the soft leather seat of Jeff's Porsche as he drove her home. The first time they'd made love, it had happened so quickly she hadn't had time to think about it, to anticipate it, or to second-guess herself. This time she did.

Not that she intended to change her mind. Something she'd dreamed of her whole life was now a reality—she and Jeff were officially involved. Of course, her fantasies had included a whole lot more than just a no-strings affair. She would be lying if she said she hadn't thought about white lace and a diamond ring. But at least they'd dispensed with the "just friends" nonsense.

Anyway, she'd meant what she said to Jeff about not being in a position to commit. She couldn't make any promises to anybody until she knew whether she had a full life ahead of her. She would never expect any man to stay with her if she found out she was sick, particularly if she had a terminal illness. That would be Jeff's worst nightmare, and it wouldn't be fair to him.

Next week, if she was given a clean bill of health after her needle biopsy, she could revive her forever-for-eternity fantasies. For now they were on ice. And if she got bad news...well, she'd already decided she would make up some excuse to break things off with Jeff. Then, after a decent interval, she would pretend she'd only just learned she had cancer.

"You're awfully quiet," Jeff said.

"Just wondering where I put those condoms I had in Dallas," she said with a laugh.

"Do we need to stop somewhere?"

"No, no. I think I can find them." And she would drive all the way to Tyler before buying condoms at the Cottonwood Drugstore. She and Jeff would generate plenty of gossip as it was.

"Do you want to get on the Pill?" he asked casually. "I've got tons of free samples at the office."

"I'll think about it." It would make sense. If she was going to be having regular sex, condoms might not be her best choice. She wanted children, but not unplanned ones.

"Is this too weird, talking so casually about birth control?"

She laughed nervously. "You got that right."

"Talking about personal stuff isn't something I excel at."

"Neither do I, apparently."

He glanced over at her. "Don't worry, I'm not likely to start dumping a lot of heavy-duty emotional stuff on you."

"No, I wouldn't expect you to. I'm the one who gets a little angsty sometimes."

Jeff reached over and caressed her cheek with his knuckles. "Hardly ever. That's one of the things I like about you, Allie. You're not a whiner."

She took that as being put on notice—he didn't want her bending his ear about personal issues, either. If she needed to confide her angst in anyone, she vowed, she would pick Anne or her mother.

Jeff pulled up into her driveway. It was very late, she realized, almost one o'clock. The street was quiet, everyone's lights out. Would her neighbors hear the rumble of Jeff's Porsche and look out to see what was going on? It didn't matter if they did, she realized. If Jeff spent the night—and she had every reason to believe he would—the neighbors would see his car parked in her driveway when they went out to get their newspapers, and her shiny new romance would suddenly become very public.

She decided she didn't really care. She'd been the spinster dentist of Cottonwood for far too long. If any of her patients decided to take their teeth elsewhere because they didn't approve of her fast morals, then so be it. She was going to live it up while she could.

She didn't bother asking Jeff if he wanted to come in. She knew he would. In fact, she'd barely gotten the front door open before he pushed her inside, then backed her up against the wall and kissed her as if he really meant it.

"Jeff!"

"I've been wanting to do this all night, ever since I saw you dancing with my brother." He pressed his mouth against hers again, more gently this time, nipping, exploring and causing her breath to come in excited gasps. "Better find those condoms," he said between his sensual assaults. "Better find a lot of them. I intend to keep you busy the rest of the night."

"Ooh, big words. Let's see if he can back them up." Allison ducked under his arm and out of his grasp, sashaying toward the bedroom with a deliberate sway to her hips.

He followed.

"I'll be right back." She ducked into the master bath, taking a peek in the mirror and groaning. She was not at her glamorous best, yet Jeff still wanted her. That was a good sign. Maybe his attraction to her wasn't completely superficial, as she'd feared.

Allison dug her travel cosmetics bag from a drawer and located the condoms. She ran a quick comb through her hair, took a swig of mouthwash, and started to dab on perfume until she remembered he didn't like it. When she reentered the bedroom, she found the covers on her bed already pulled back. Jeff lay there against her floral sheets wearing a confident grin—and nothing else. The only light on was the one by the bed, which cast him in a soft spotlight.

"You gonna ditch those clothes," he asked in a lazy voice, "or do I have to do it for you?"

Could she manage a sensual striptease? She'd never done anything so blatant in her life. She'd spent too many years feeling ashamed of her body to flaunt it so brazenly. Taking a deep breath, she kicked off her espadrilles, then unzipped her denim skirt and shimmied out of it. At least the lights were low. Her method didn't have a whole lot of style or grace, but Jeff didn't seem to care.

He watched approvingly as she pulled her knit shirt over her head. It got stuck on her earring, and she took a few moments to unhook it, giggling nervously. "Guess I'm not ready to audition for Baby Doll's," she said, referring to a strip club in the next town over.

"I bet a lot of men would pay good money to see you strip."

She tossed her shirt aside, standing before Jeff in her baby-blue camisole and bikini underwear. "Fortunately, you don't have to. What a savings."

He sat up and crooked a finger at her. She approached, her stomach swooping with anticipation. She felt completely vulnerable when he looked at her like that. She came close enough that he could touch her, and he did, spanning her waist with his hands, then smoothing his palms over her hips to cup her bottom. Then he hooked his fingers into the waist of her panties and slowly slid them down her legs.

Allison thought her heart was going to beat its way out of her chest. She started to pull off the camisole, but he stopped her.

"Leave it. I like how that looks on you."

Score another point for Hollywood Lingerie, she thought dazedly as he pulled her onto the bed.

Their lovemaking in Dallas had been wildly intense and over far too quickly. This time, Jeff took his time, discovering what pleased her, showing her what he liked, which caresses made him purr and which ones drove him out of his skin.

"I'm putting a lot of power in your hands, showing you this stuff," he said as he nuzzled the cleavage between her breasts. "You can put me completely under your control any time you want, just by touching me…here.'' He guided her hand to a spot on his inner thigh that very nearly paralyzed him with delight.

Powerful stuff indeed.

Allison thought she might expire from wanting until she had to beg Jeff to put her out of her misery. This he happily did. She reached an incredible peak of ecstasy that left her mindless. And just when she'd caught her breath and decided she could not feel any happier, he brought her back to another peak.

''That's…that's impossible!'' she blurted out after she'd again caught her breath.

''No, just difficult. Only trained experts should attempt this. Don't try it at home.''

''I *am* at home. And I don't want to even think about your training,'' she muttered as she snuggled close to him, enjoying the aftermath almost as much as the lovemaking itself. Then, after a pause of a few seconds, she added, ''Can we do it again?''

He laughed. ''I'm a trained expert, not a superhero. Give me a few minutes.''

She did, but only a few, insisting he live up to his earlier bragging. Now that she had him in her bed, she didn't intend to forgo one single pleasure she might derive from their being together. The fact that she had no clue when their relationship would end lent a certain desperation to their sexual activities, at least in Allison's point of view. That sharper edge was pleasurable, yet painful, too.

Jeff finally gave out about four in the morning, resisting Allison's attempts to cajole him into activity. In truth, she was pretty worn-out herself. She just wanted the satisfaction of him being the one to tire out first.

With a sigh of supreme satisfaction, she snuggled under the covers, her head on his shoulder, feeling the deepest contentment she'd ever experienced.

She didn't sleep long, less than three hours. Dawn came late this time of year, but it came all the same. As the first dim light of morning crept into the room, Allison's contentment was replaced with a piercing longing. She wanted this thing with Jeff to last—forever. She'd always wanted happily ever after, but now, after experiencing the real thing rather than just a fantasy, her wanting had increased a hundredfold.

She knew the odds were against them. Jeff had never stayed interested in any one woman for longer than a few weeks. Why would she affect him any differently? And even if she did manage to hold his attention for longer, there was her health to consider. Bad news from her doctor could throw a king-size wrench into the works.

She'd thought she could compromise. She'd even told Jeff that when he wanted to dump her, she would let him go without a whimper. But now she just didn't know how she would honor that promise. The magnitude of her potential loss had grown astronomically in the past few hours. Having him here, in her bed at home, was so much more real than sharing an anonymous bed in a hotel room.

She trembled at the mere thought of having him, then losing him. What if she'd made a terrible decision?

JEFF AWOKE to the smell of coffee. It took a few moments for him to remember where he was. When he did, he stretched and smiled, recalling a few of the more savory details of last night's lovemaking. He was sorry to note that he was alone in bed, but judging by the slant of the sun coming through the curtains, it was late. Allison was an early riser.

Allison was also a huge surprise. He'd known her his whole life, yet she seemed like a completely new person to him. Whatever her experience or lack thereof, she had instincts where he was concerned. She did things to him that sent him into orbit, and most of the time he didn't even have to show her what he liked. He seemed to have some kind of sixth sense where her body was concerned, too. He always seemed to know where to touch and how, and her sighs and moans of pleasure were a reward unto themselves.

Jeff dragged himself out of bed. He checked his beeper—by some miracle, no messages. This was his dad's weekend to take emergencies, but that didn't mean some stubborn patients didn't insist on trying to get hold of him. Usually he obliged by calling back. It always felt good if he could reassure someone over the phone or give them some first-aid advice.

"Allison?"

No answer. He walked down the hall toward the kitchen and found a note on the coffeemaker: "Went riding. Back around ten. Help yourself to coffee, and if you're still here when I get back, I'll make breakfast—*healthy* breakfast."

Well, hell, he should have known she wouldn't forgo her regular Saturday ride just to loll around in bed with him. She usually met some biking friends and they rode for about fifty miles. She'd tried to cajole him a time or two into buying a bike and giving the sport a try, but he'd resisted.

Maybe he'd been too stubborn, he thought as he stepped into the shower. If he'd taken an interest in Allison's hobby, he could be with her now instead of wandering around her empty house and using her shower and her girly smelling soap.

He should be glad she wasn't clinging to him. Most of the women he dated became very needy and demanding of his time once they went to bed together, figuring they had some claim to him. Apparently, Allison was going to go on behaving just as she always did.

Healthy breakfast. As a doctor, he approved. As a normal human, he wanted his full ration of fat and cholesterol. He decided to leave before she got back and go to the Miracle Café for biscuits and gravy. He would write Allison a cheery note, just as she'd done him, and then he'd call her later.

But he was still there, sitting on her sofa drinking her damned decaffeinated coffee and reading a bicycle magazine, when she returned from her bike ride all hot and damp and sexy.

He endured a yogurt-strawberry smoothie and some kind of cereal that tasted like sawdust, and he didn't even complain.

His behavior was mildly disturbing.

ALLISON NOTICED Jeff wince as he drank the smoothie she'd made for him. Either he really didn't like the taste and was just being polite, or he had a bum tooth.

"Do you have a tooth that's bothering you?" she asked point blank.

"Just a little sensitive to the cold."

"Better let me check it out. You might have a hairline crack, and it's better to deal with it now than have the tooth break unexpectedly." She knew better than to suggest Jeff might have a cavity. He was very proud of the fact that he had perfect teeth.

"It's nothing."

"How long has it been bothering you?"

He shrugged uneasily. "Couple of months."

"Jeff Hardison, you know better."

"Oh, all right. How about Thursday afternoon? That's when I normally play tennis, but I could skip this once."

"I'm sure that's fine. Call Jenny—oh, no, wait, I won't be in the office all day Thursday."

"Really? You never take time off. What's up?"

"I just wanted a day off," she said, probably too

defensively. "I'm driving into Dallas to go, um, shopping."

"Shopping?" He looked at her as if she'd grown tentacles. "You hate shopping. You buy everything from catalogues."

What he said used to be true. She'd been loath to face department-store dressing rooms, with their all-seeing mirrors and harsh light that magnified her cellulite. But shopping with Anne had been sort of fun, now that she didn't have to avert her gaze so much. She also liked the greater selection she had, now that she wore a more mainstream size.

Shopping was not her objective next Thursday, however. That was when she'd scheduled her needle biopsy. She'd rearranged appointments so she could have the whole day—in case she got bad news. She didn't want to have to come back to her office and weep on her patients.

"I've learned to enjoy it," she said simply. "Tell you what. I'll see you after hours any other day this week."

"Okay. I'll check my calendar and call you." He continued to study her over the rim of his glass—suspiciously, she thought, although maybe she was just being paranoid.

They lingered over coffee and the newspaper, but Allison felt a pinch in her happiness, now that she'd been reminded of her doctor's appointment. She loved that she and Jeff were so comfortable with each other, like long-time lovers might be. She hated that he would be leaving soon, and she had no idea what he thought about last night or when they might spend the night together again. Still, there was no way she would bring it up. Jeff had told her a million times how he hated clingy women, so she did not intend to act like one—even if today she felt like one inside.

Chapter Nine

"Supper's on," announced Sally, Jeff's soon-to-be stepgrandmother, the following Sunday at the Hardison Ranch. Once Pete and Sally had gotten together, the wiry older woman had quickly become part of the family. Unable to stomach the lousy meals thrown together by the Hardison men for their weekly family get-together, she'd taken over cooking.

"I want to sit next to Uncle Jeff," announced Sam, Jonathan's eight-year-old.

Not to be outdone, six-year-old Kristin grabbed Allison's hand. "I want to sit next to you, Aunt Allison."

Allison gave Jeff a surprised look, then quickly recovered. "Of course you can sit next to me, sweetheart," she said, then whispered to Jeff, "Since when did I become an aunt?"

"I had nothing to do with it," Jeff whispered back with a shrug. He marveled at his niece and nephew's sudden devotion as they all played musical chairs. In fact, the whole family was treating him differently since he and Allison had become a couple. It was as if he'd suddenly become respectable.

"Heard there was a set-to at the Chatsworths' fish fry after I went home," Pete mentioned casually as he served himself a slice of country ham and redeye gravy.

Uh-oh, here it comes, Jeff thought.

"You missed a good show, Granddad," Wade said, thoroughly enjoying the fact that for once he wasn't the one in trouble. "Jeff thought Jon was moving in on his territory and popped him one right in the mouth."

"A lucky punch," Jon said good-naturedly, touching his tender lip. "He took me by surprise."

Pete looked at Jeff—not condemning but appraising. Jeff felt like squirming, but he calmly served Allison some peas before putting a spoonful on his own plate.

"I don't approve of fighting," Pete said, "you know that."

"Yes, sir," Jeff said automatically.

"But defending a woman's honor, that's different."

"Not that my honor needed defending," Allison hastily added. "But I suppose his heart was in the right place."

"Just not his fist," Jon said, chuckling.

Pete nodded, then looked at Allison. "Allie, girl, it's a good man who'll make a fool of himself for love. Obviously, you don't think too poorly of his actions, or you wouldn't be with him tonight."

Allison blushed. Probably the word *love* had disconcerted her, Jeff thought, just as it had him. But as long as Pete wasn't going to harangue him for public brawling, he wasn't going to object.

That was all that was said on the matter, but Jeff couldn't help but notice that Sally cut him an extra-large piece of carrot cake. He even caught his father watching him more closely than usual, a faint expression of approval in his eye.

Imagine, he'd suddenly become a hero by turning himself into a fool over a woman.

The story was a little different when Allison invited him to dinner at her parents' house three days later. Jeff had run tame at the Cranes' house since he was a kid. Barbara, Allison's mother, had always been kind to him, but the Reverend Lester Crane made his mouth go dry. It was a bit nerve-racking to sit across the dinner table from the man who preached fire and brimstone at the pulpit of Jeff's church every Sunday.

Even as an adult, Jeff hadn't entirely gotten over being nervous around Mr. Crane. He had bulging, almost-black eyes that seemed to see right through Jeff, even if they were discussing football or cars or lawn fertilizers.

At this particular dinner, Jeff was more jittery than usual. Unless the Cranes were deaf and blind, they'd heard the gossip about the brawl at the Chatsworths' fish fry, and the reasons behind it. They also no doubt knew of Allison's long-standing, unrequited crush on Jeff.

"Do they know about us?" Jeff asked Allison when they had a moment alone before dinner. Jonas, the Cranes' Chihuahua, pranced at Jeff's feet. He scooped up the little dog and stroked it absently, feeling a certain kinship with the nervous animal.

"Have I told my father, the preacher, that we're sleeping together?" she asked, surprised. "No. Have they figured it out? Probably. They listen to gossip just like everyone else."

Jeff felt suddenly warm and wished someone would crack open a window. Jonas, seeming concerned, stood up on his pencil-thin hind legs and licked Jeff's face.

Barbara was cordial as ever, having fixed Jeff's favorite—chicken-fried steak and mashed potatoes. Though both of Allison's parents were thin as birds, Barbara cooked like this every night.

Before anyone lifted a fork, however, Mr. Crane had to say a prayer. By now, Jeff was used to this. No quickly mumbled stock blessing at the Cranes' dinner table—the minister sometimes pontificated until the dinner was growing cold.

Tonight was no exception. Everyone joined hands, and Lester began his blessing. "Honor us with your presence, O Lord, and bless this food that graces our table through your bounty. Know that we are grateful for the abundance in our lives and the love and friendship that brings us together at this table."

So far, so good, Jeff thought. Love and friendship.

"Help us each to live the good Christian lives You intend for us," Lester continued, "to follow the path of giving that will please You. Remind us daily to live by the Golden Rule, and to respect each other.''

At this point Lester usually asked for something for each person at the table. ''Bless the food my lovely wife, Barbara, has prepared, and bring peace to her sewing circle. Let our brother Jeff practice his healing arts with your assistance and blessing.'' Lester opened his eyes and stared directly at Jeff, who always had trouble keeping his eyes closed during prayer. ''And please, dear Lord, bless my only offspring Allison, and give her the wisdom to make choices in accordance with your will, and to choose the company of those who will not lead her astray. As for myself, your humble servant, help me to control my temper, which has been strained as of late. Amen.''

''Amen,'' the rest of them said.

Jeff glanced over at Allison. She was trying not to laugh at her father's less-than-subtle warning. Jeff bit his tongue.

The rest of the meal proceeded smoothly enough, though every once in a while Jeff caught Lester staring at him.

Later, as he and Allison walked out to his car in the driveway, she finally let loose with her laughter. ''My dad, subtle as a charging rhinoceros.''

Jeff just shook his head. ''I don't know, Allie. This is really bizarre.''

''Why? Hasn't any girl's father ever given you the third degree?''

"Not that I can remember." The reason for that, he realized, was that he'd never enmeshed himself in the family of any woman he dated. If one of them ever invited him to a family gathering, he made it a rule to turn her down, because he didn't want the hassle of having to prove his worthiness to relatives he cared nothing about. In fact, being invited home to meet the family was a sure sign that a woman was getting too serious—and it was time to move on.

Now he found himself caring, a lot. He wanted Lester Crane to look on him with fondness, rather than warning and censure. The feelings were strange and alien, but he told himself this was all his own fault. He'd told Allison he was ready for a more mature relationship. Did mature relationships mean worrying about what some girl's parents thought about him?

"Dad's bark is worse than his bite," Allison said. "I'm still his little girl, and he's not comfortable with the idea of sharing me with any other man. He'll calm down, once he realizes you're not a threat."

"I hope so."

She suddenly turned serious. "This has gotten more complicated than you were bargaining for. Am I right?"

He nodded, then smiled. "I'm a tough guy, I can take it."

She smiled back. "I was hoping you'd say that." She looked at her watch. "Hey, it's early. Want to go to my office and let me X-ray your tooth?"

Somehow he'd managed to conveniently forget about his promise to let Allison and her tools of torture into his mouth. She'd seldom cajoled him into her dentist's chair. He'd been blessed with good teeth—he'd never had even one cavity—so he didn't take her dire warnings seriously.

He waved away her suggestion. "It can wait. Anyway, the tooth hardly bothers me at all." Just when he drank something very cold. Or hot. Or if he chewed down hard on something. "I have something much more interesting in mind than dentistry."

She gave him a sultry look. "Is that so?"

He promptly forgot about Mr. Crane and sensitive teeth and drove his car back to Allison's house, where he made good his promise. After a particularly intense session of lovemaking, he lay with Allison in his arms, filled with a sense of rightness. He could endure all the family pressures in the world, if only he had the promise of making love with Allison to look forward to.

His feeling of contentment lasted until the following morning, when she didn't jump out of bed before dawn as she usually did.

"No bike ride today?" he asked.

"I'm sleeping in. This is my day off, remember?"

Oh, yes, the infamous shopping trip to Dallas. "Want some company? I only have a couple of appointments this morning, and Dad could cover for me."

"You want to come shopping with me?" she asked in a decidedly panicked tone of voice.

''I want to sleep in with you,'' he corrected her. If there was anyone who hated shopping more than Allison, it was Jeff. He nuzzled her neck and reached to caress her breast through her silk pajamas, but she shied away from him.

''No, I really should get going,'' she said, suddenly all business. She jumped out of bed as if she'd been doused with cold water, and darted to the bathroom. Moments later he heard the shower running.

Something weird was going on. He couldn't quite put his finger on it, but something about this shopping trip to Dallas didn't ring true.

Jeff quickly showered in the other bathroom, then put on the clean clothes he'd brought with him. He and Allison had learned to make themselves at home at each other's houses long before they'd started sleeping together, but he resisted any urge to leave a few toiletries in her medicine cabinet or hang a couple of spare shirts in her closet. Working on the theory that familiarity bred contempt, he made it a policy not to get that cozy with any woman. Nothing like a lover's dirty laundry or antiperspirant to suck the mystique right out of a relationship.

They rendezvoused in the kitchen, where Jeff toasted a bagel for himself and Allison sliced up fruit to put in her granola.

''So what are you shopping for?'' he asked casually.

She shrugged. ''Whatever strikes my fancy.''

''When do you think you'll be back? No, wait, let me rephrase that,'' he added quickly when he realized he sounded like a jealous husband checking up on his wife. He hated it when anyone questioned *his* comings and goings, even if the interest was prompted only by polite curiosity. "I thought we might go to dinner in Tyler tonight. Will you be back in time?"

She hesitated before answering. "I'd really like to just take the night off, if you don't mind. Could we make a date for Friday instead?"

He forced a smile. "Sure." Then he bolted down the rest of his bagel, claimed he had an early appointment and got the hell out of there. Because a terrible thought had occurred to him, and he wanted to escape from Allison before he could voice it. Was she meeting someone in Dallas, a man, perhaps? He recalled the mysterious appointment she'd kept during the convention, right after they'd made love the first time.

Did she have a boyfriend?

He'd always assumed Allison told him everything, but if she had a boyfriend, maybe she'd kept quiet about it. She was looking like such a hot number these days, it was easy to imagine her attracting men in any city she chose. A lover in Dallas would be suitably discreet.

He halted his wild imaginings. He was being ridiculous, wasn't he? Allison wasn't the type to carry on a secret, torrid affair, especially not when she was dating him. Then again, their affair had materialized so suddenly, maybe she hadn't had time to break it off with this other man. Maybe she was going to Dallas to meet him and say goodbye.

Certainly that was a more palatable possibility than the idea that she would continue to carry on with Mr. X, but the whole idea that she was involved with another man made Jeff feel as if his bones had caught fire.

He and Allison had made no commitments to each other, he reminded himself. She was free to see other men, just as he could see other women if he wanted. But the thought that she would had never occurred to him.

ALLISON SAT in the waiting room in Stephanie's office, working her way through a stack of old magazines and awaiting the results of her needle biopsy. Stephanie had told her she could go home and the results would be given to her as soon as they came in. But Allison felt too nervous to drive. The lab was supposed to analyze the results of the tests sometime that afternoon, and she'd decided she wasn't moving from this spot until they made good on their promise.

The procedure itself hadn't been bad. Stephanie had used a local anesthetic, and since Allison was around needles all the time it didn't bother her. Then Stephanie had inserted a needle into the mass in her breast and sucked out a small amount to be studied by a pathologist for signs of cancer. It was over almost before it started.

Now that the anesthetic was wearing off there was

some discomfort, and Allison expected she would have a bruise, but that was it. She was already trying to figure out how she would explain the bruise to Jeff, because surely he would notice. He noticed everything about her. He'd found a heart-shaped freckle on her back that she hadn't even known she had.

After two excruciating hours of waiting, a nurse called Allison back to Stephanie's office. Stephanie was there, her expression neutral, and Allison's heart sank. Surely if it was good news, her friend would be smiling.

"Tell me," Allison said without preamble. "It's bad, isn't it?"

"No, it's not bad," Stephanie said. "But it's not good, either."

"Well, what is it, then?"

"Inconclusive. Sometimes you just can't get definitive results with this type of test. Unfortunately, that's what's happened in your case."

"So what do we do now?" Allison swallowed back the tears that threatened. She'd been so sure she would get an answer this afternoon, one way or another. Now there was just more uncertainty.

"I think you should have the lump removed."

Surgery. Allison closed her eyes a moment to absorb the reality. The only surgery she'd ever had was when she had her wisdom teeth removed. "Are we talking a hospital stay?"

"It can probably be handled as day surgery. Of course, someone will have to be there with you, so they can drive you home afterward. It would be even better if you could stay in town with someone overnight, so you wouldn't have to deal with the long drive back to Cottonwood.''

''My aunt lives in town,'' Allison said, thinking aloud. ''My mother could come with me for the surgery, and we could stay and visit with relatives.''

Stephanie nodded her approval. ''Then let's schedule it as soon as possible. I've got a couple of surgeons I work with who are excellent. Let me see when they can get you in.''

ALLISON WAS BONE TIRED when she drove home late that afternoon. Her muscles felt as if she'd been systematically beaten. She knew her soreness was a result of the tension she'd been holding in her body, and she looked forward to a long soak in a hot bath.

Her surgery was scheduled for next Wednesday in the day-surgery unit at Woodside Memorial Medical Center. There was still a chance, however, that she would have to stay overnight. Her small tumor would be sent to the pathology lab for immediate examination. If evidence of cancer was discovered, the surgeon would have to go in again and take out more tissue to ensure that all of the malignancy was removed.

She hadn't yet decided whether she would let the physician remove her entire breast. Although some said this procedure would offer her the very highest chances of survival, it was a highly personal decision, and neither Stephanie nor the surgeon, a Dr.

Evans, were pushing her into it. They said she needed to weigh the pros and cons and decide herself. She would talk it over with her mother and Anne.

As she turned onto her street, she almost took out a row of her neighbor's shrubs. Jeff's Porsche was sitting in front of her house. What was he doing there? Though they'd been dropping by each other's homes unannounced for years, this was different. She'd specifically told him she wanted to spend tonight at home resting—alone.

Funny, but a couple of weeks ago her heart would be leaping for joy at the sight of that Porsche. But tonight Jeff's appearance meant something completely different. It meant she would have to lie, to act, to put on a happy face when she felt like warmed-over oatmeal. She loved Jeff more than any person on the face of the earth, and she hated deceiving him.

Allison considered driving right past her place and on to her parents' house. They were anxious to hear how her visit to Dallas went, and she could spend the night there and avoid Jeff awhile longer. But unfortunately Jeff was sitting on her front porch swing, and he spotted her Toyota long before she'd reached the middle of the block, where her house sat.

She was surprised at how...devoted he'd become. She'd never imagined his being so attentive toward any lover.

She pulled into the driveway, waving and pasting

on a smile, then pulling around to the garage. How was she going to do this? Just that one smile made her face hurt.

She entered the house through the garage door into the kitchen, where Jeff met her with a kiss.

"Do you have packages to carry in?"

"Hmm?"

"I assume a whole day's worth of shopping in Dallas produced more than this." He pointed to the tiny shopping bag she carried in one hand, which contained a bottle of her favorite moisturizer. She'd stopped at Neiman's, which was the only place she knew of that carried the stuff, before her doctor's appointment, so that at least her claim to be in Dallas "shopping" wouldn't be a lie.

"Oh, um, actually, this is all I bought."

His face radiated incredulity. "That's it?"

She shrugged. "Some days you just can't find anything that appeals to you. Men don't understand shopping at all." She hung her purse and jacket on a hook by the garage door, hoping he would take her explanation at face value.

He seemed to, at least for now, but he gave her a funny look.

"What are you doing here, anyway?" she asked as she put the kettle on. She intended to have a nice cup of herbal tea, which she'd been looking forward to all day.

"Now that's gratitude for you. I know you said you didn't want to go out, so I brought dinner to you. KFC. It's in the oven, keeping warm."

She mustered a smile. "Since when did you become so thoughtful?" It wasn't unusual for her to spontaneously fix Jeff dinner or surprise him in some other way, but Jeff—and men in general, she'd discovered—didn't often reciprocate. It wasn't that they were thoughtless or didn't care. Their brains just didn't sail down those channels. Thus, Jeff's gesture was doubly surprising, as well as troubling. She figured he intended to stick around. And for the first time in her life that she could remember, she didn't want him to.

"Not thoughtful," he corrected her. "Completely selfish." As she reached into the cupboard for the tea, he put his arms around her from behind. "You've spoiled me. I didn't want to spend the evening alone."

Now she really was shocked. Jeff Hardison was...clinging. Ordinarily she would be thrilled to her bone marrow. But now, of all times?

Tell him, a strange voice inside her urged. *He really does care for you. Tell him the hell you're going through. Let him hold you and comfort you.*

But it was because he did care for her that she couldn't unload on him. He'd hurt so badly when his mother was ill with the very same disease Allison might have. She knew the terrible pictures that had been flashing through her imagination ever since she'd found the lump. She knew Jeff's imagination would conjure even worse images, because of what he'd experienced firsthand. She couldn't put him through that.

She just couldn't.

When Jeff's arm inadvertently brushed her sore breast, she gasped sharply.

"What?" The concern in his voice almost did her in.

"Nothing." She wiggled out of his embrace. "Just a stomach cramp. I've been having them all day. That's probably why I couldn't find anything I wanted to buy. It's hard to spend money when you don't feel well."

"Then why didn't you come home?"

She shrugged. "Dogged determination, I guess. And the eternal hope that the perfect sweater at the perfect price would fall off a hanger at my feet."

"There's a stomach bug going around. Dad and I saw three cases today alone."

"I'm sure it's nothing," she said, waving away his concern. "Just nerves or something."

"What do you have to be nervous about?"

"I don't know." His interrogation was trying her patience. Couldn't he just let it go? "Sometimes I get nervous about life in general." There, now. What could be closer to the truth?

"Allison. I've known you a long time, and you've never been the nervous, jumpy type."

"Then you don't know every single thing about me, do you? I get nervous all the time. I just don't admit to it." And her nerves were becoming more frayed by the minute. With trembling hands she poured boiling water into a mug with a teabag. She hadn't bothered to ask Jeff if he wanted any tea—he hated the stuff.

"They make medicine for that."

"Oh, no, you don't. You're not going to pump me full of pills. Can we just…eat dinner?" If she'd been hungry when she walked into the house, she wasn't now. But she figured the sooner she could get through dinner, the sooner she could claim a headache and crawl into bed—alone.

"Okay, okay. You know I'm just worried about you, right?"

She managed a smile of gratitude—genuine, this time. Yes, she knew Jeff cared, and his concern warmed her like a down quilt on a winter night. In fact, she had high hopes that his fondness for her would eventually lead to love. But ironically this one night, the fact he cared was like a splinter in her foot, reminding her with each step that she might have to hurt him.

Allison found some leftover baked beans and coleslaw in her refrigerator. She warmed the beans in the microwave while she set the kitchen table. Jeff served them each two pieces from the bucket of warm chicken, and for a few minutes they maintained a scene of cozy domesticity that was comforting to Allison.

If only she didn't have this *thing* to worry about, which was becoming a huge black cloud blotting out the sunshine.

Jeff got up and went to the oven, where the rest of the chicken was keeping warm. "Do you want another piece? I think there's only one breast left. Speak up if you want it. Otherwise it's mine. You know how I love breasts.'' He waggled his eyebrows.

Allison couldn't answer. She'd been doing fine, until he'd mentioned that word. His suggestive joke was lost on her as her throat closed and her eyes brimmed with tears.

She blotted her eyes with her napkin, hoping Jeff wouldn't notice, but there were more tears behind the ones she dried. As Jeff returned to the table with two pieces of chicken—one of them definitely a breast—Allison knew she couldn't sit there a second longer. She bolted from the table, making a beeline for the half bath off the kitchen, hoping against hope Jeff wouldn't think her behavior too odd.

No such luck.

''Allison!'' He was only a few steps behind her, but she managed to slam and lock the door before he caught up with her. ''Allison, what in the hell is wrong with you?''

''Jeff, could you...just please...go home?'' she gasped out between sobs. She'd been fighting the urge to cry ever since Stephanie had given her the ambiguous news about her test results, but she'd told herself not to, that crying never solved anything, that she'd only work herself up into a state and make things worse. She'd thought she had control of herself.

Apparently not, because she was sobbing like a three-year-old. Why now, of all times? She wished she'd gotten this out of her system in the privacy of her car, on the way home.

"I'm not going home until you come out of there and tell me what's wrong."

"It's nothing!" she insisted. "It's hormones. PMS." She felt guilty falling back on that old chestnut, but desperate times called for desperate measures.

"Bull. You've never suffered PMS a day in your life."

"How do you know? I wouldn't have told you about it."

"Well, if that's all it is, then come out."

"No. You hate crying women. You've told me that."

"I believe I said I don't like it when women try to manipulate me by crying. Clearly that is not the case here."

"I don't want you to see me looking like this. My face is all puffy and blotchy."

"Do you think I care about that?"

"Yes! Jeff, please. I really need to spend the evening alone. Tomorrow we can go out, do anything you want. But tonight I just need you to…go away."

There was a long silence.

"Jeff?"

Nothing. Allison opened the door and peeked out. He was gone.

Chapter Ten

Jeff drove home, probably too fast, with a sick feeling in his stomach. Allison had told him to go away. She'd never said that to him.

In fact, no one had ever said that to him, except maybe his brothers when he'd deliberately provoked them.

True, he and Allison had spent an unusual amount of time together over the past week. Once they'd admitted they wanted to be together, they couldn't get enough of each other. At least, that was how he felt. He'd thought she felt the same. He was pretty good at reading between the lines, at understanding body language and tone of voice.

Anyway, in any relationship he'd ever been in— and he was ashamed to admit there'd been at least a dozen—he was always the first to start feeling smothered. He was always the first to back off, to claim to need his space or whatever the current phraseology was. He'd never been the recipient of such sentiments.

He felt a twinge of guilt for all the women he'd

perhaps caused to feel the way he felt right now, which was lousy. But he couldn't waste too much time on remorse. He had other things to figure out— like what the hell was wrong with Allison.

Something was screwy about her trip to Dallas. What woman spent an entire day shopping and returned home with nothing to show for it but a bag the size of a lunch sack? He had no choice but to conclude she was doing something besides shopping in Dallas. Which led him to an earlier suspicion, which he'd previously dismissed as ridiculous but was gaining more and more credence.

Could Allison have another lover? More to the point, could she be so devious as to carry on with some other man at the same time she was seeing Jeff, and not tell him?

Sure, they'd agreed to "no strings." In Jeff's book, that meant no commitments, no implied future trips to the altar, no diamond rings expected. He still didn't feel free to have sex with other women. He'd never dreamed Allison's definition was so different.

By the time he reached his own house, he'd whipped himself into a frenzy of jealousy. How could she treat him this way? How could she have so little respect for their friendship that she would deceive him, that she would cheat on him?

He felt that he needed to tell someone, to get some sane person's perspective on this. But normally, if he had a problem, he would call Allison. Clearly that wasn't an option.

Tomorrow, though, he would confront her. He

would demand that she tell him the truth. And once she confessed, he would tell her he couldn't tolerate her seeing other men. He didn't care for ultimatums, but in this case he felt one was warranted.

ALLISON SLEPT HARD, and by morning she felt more like herself. Her performance in front of Jeff last night seemed like a bad dream, but as soon as she talked to him, she would set him straight. She would apologize for her emotional outburst and ask if he would kindly put it out of his memory.

Her steady stream of patients buoyed her spirits immensely. She put on a cheerful face for them, and pretty soon she actually was cheerful. But by noon she realized Jeff hadn't called.

Had she hurt his feelings last night? She'd told him to go away, and that wasn't very nice. She would have to make it up to him, and she could think of several intriguing ways.

She ate a takeout roast-beef sandwich for lunch, holed up in her office doing paperwork. A few minutes before her first afternoon patient, she called Jeff.

"Hi." That was the sum total of Jeff's greeting.

"Hi, yourself. Oh, Jeff, I'm really sorry for acting like such an imbecile last night."

"Apology accepted."

But it didn't sound like it, she thought. Jeff could put sunshine into his voice when he wanted to. Now he sounded like an Arctic blizzard.

"Are we on for tonight?" She injected false cheer

into her voice, trying to pretend everything was normal.

"If you like."

"Let me fix you dinner."

"All right."

They arranged a time, and when Allison hung up, she felt shaken, and for the first time in a long time she felt unsure of her appeal. Was this the beginning of the end? Sure, Jeff had seemed entranced with her over the past week, but she knew how short his attention span was when it came to women. Had her disgraceful crying episode last night turned him off completely?

She had at least one more evening with him. Maybe if she made everything perfect, then became a sex goddess in bed...

No. She was not going to start thinking like that. She was not going to become one of those pathetic women who constantly worried she would lose her man, who stretched themselves in every direction trying to maintain interest, who begged for morsels of affection, which they lived on for weeks. Jeff would have to accept the person she was—and that included putting up with an occasional, irrational crying jag.

After all, she'd warned him away. She'd known she wouldn't be at her best last night, and he'd chosen to ignore her warnings. If he couldn't handle the consequences, if he was that intolerant of her lapse of grace and emotional control, then she didn't need to be involved with him.

It felt strange, pondering the idea of letting him go, when she'd spent most of her life imagining how ideal her romance with Jeff would be. In fact, it tied her heart into a big knot. But she'd seen other women lose themselves in one-way relationships, and she was determined not to do that.

Allison decided to make beef Stroganoff, a dish she and Jeff both enjoyed. She stopped at the store on the way home and bought the ingredients, then dashed across the county line to buy a bottle of wine.

While the noodles cooked, she changed into blue satin underthings, noting the unattractive bruise on her breast. Maybe if she kept the lights dim, Jeff wouldn't notice.

If they got that far.

Were the candles in the dining room a tad too much? Nah. Jeff would get a kick out of it.

She hoped.

Jeff rang the doorbell promptly at seven. She greeted him with a smile, which quickly faded when she saw the look on his face. Was this really her easygoing Jeff?

"I hope you're hungry," she said breezily as she led him into the kitchen. "I've cooked enough for an army, or at least a Little League team."

No response.

"I bought some of that Keystone Vineyards burgundy you like so much. It's breathing on the counter there." She nodded toward the open bottle, which she'd driven seven miles out of her way to find. "Would you do the honors?"

"I'm not really thirsty."

Well, at least she'd gotten him to speak.

"Would you pour me some, then?" She turned to face him squarely, her arms crossed. "And while you're at it, you want to tell me what's gotten your nose so out of joint? I apologized for last night. I know you don't care for histrionics, but, jeez, cut me a break. That's the first time I've cried in front of you since tenth grade, when Kelly Binford called me a pig and you—"

"You getting emotional in front of me is not the issue," he said, ignoring the wine. "The issue is that you lied to me."

The kitchen felt suddenly very close, as if all the oxygen had been sucked out of it. "Who told you?" she whispered.

"No one told me. No one had to. I know you as well as I know anyone on this earth, Allie, and I know damn well you weren't shopping in Dallas. Which you've just admitted, thank you very much."

Then he didn't know. She relaxed slightly, took a steadying breath, then grabbed the bottle of wine and poured a glass for herself, since it didn't appear Jeff would do it for her.

"I also have a pretty good idea what you were doing in Dallas," he said.

"Oh?" She took a sip of the wine. It burned all the way down her throat.

"But I want to hear it from you."

"Hear what? Okay, you caught me. I was robbing banks."

He looked away from her, and she realized he was truly in distress over her lack of honesty. She didn't owe him any explanations, but she shouldn't be cavalier about this.

"I'm sorry. What is it you think I was doing?"

"Seeing someone."

"Seeing—you mean, like a *man?*" So that was what this was about? Allison could have laughed with joy, though she wisely held herself in check. Jeff was jealous of an imaginary boyfriend. "Oh, Jeff, that's preposterous." Why would she need any other man when she had Jeff?

"It doesn't seem preposterous to me. You disappeared one whole afternoon when we were in Dallas for the convention. Then you drive there again, alone, and spend the whole day. You come home with almost nothing to show for your 'shopping,' and you're an emotional wreck. It adds up."

"Jeff, I can assure you, there is no man in Dallas."

"Then what were you doing there? And don't try to tell me you were at the mall. I'm not that stupid."

She sighed and turned to the stove to check on her sauce, trying to collect her thoughts. He was right to be angry. She shouldn't have lied. In the past, the only thing she'd ever been less than honest about with Jeff was her true feelings for him.

"You're right," she finally said. "I wasn't shopping all day. I was attending to a personal matter."

"What kind of—"

"I can't talk about it. But it's nothing that involves you."

Jeff's immediate reaction was concern. "Are you in some kind of legal trouble? Or financial?"

"No and no. Jeff, I'm asking you to leave it alone. Forget about it." She held his gaze for several tense seconds. Finally he looked away, his expression revealing his inner conflict. She knew he was debating whether to pursue the subject further or let it drop, as she'd requested.

He poured himself a glass of wine and sat down at the kitchen table. "Do you need any help with dinner?"

Allison allowed herself a full breath for the first time in several minutes. "You can get the salad dressing out of the fridge. Everything else is under control."

He stood and headed for the refrigerator, then inexplicably stopped in the middle of the kitchen, like someone had hit him with a freeze gun.

"Jeff?"

"You never kept secrets from me before. Why now? Why, now that we've become physically involved, can you no longer trust me?"

Oh, hell, he wasn't going to let this drop. She wanted to tell him the truth, she really did. And he did have a point. Before they'd become lovers, she probably would have confided her health concerns to him, because she'd always told him everything.

But she couldn't confide in him now. She could not stand the thought that he might stay with her out of pity, out of misplaced loyalty or merely because he did not want to look and feel lower than a snake's belly for abandoning his new girlfriend at the first sign of trouble.

"I can't tell you," she said firmly, trying to soften her implacable stance with a smile. "And no amount of reasoning or bullying on your part will make me change my mind."

"Fine." As he walked to the table and grabbed his leather jacket from off the back of the chair where he'd draped it, Allison felt her world crashing down around her ears.

He was leaving her.

"Jeff, what is with you?" she objected, following him toward the door.

"Maybe this was all a very bad idea," he said, shoving his arms into the sleeves of his jacket. "I know we said 'no strings,' but I didn't think that meant no trust, as well." With that he stormed out.

Allison returned to the kitchen on shaky legs and turned off the flame under her beef Stroganoff, then sank to her kitchen floor. For the second evening in a row she wept until she ran out of tears.

"WHERE'S ALLISON?" Sally Enderlin asked the moment Jeff cleared the threshold at the ranch on Sunday. The mouthwatering scent of homemade chili wafted from the kitchen.

"She couldn't come," Jeff said, having vowed to dodge any and all questions regarding Allison. His feelings about their breakup were still too raw. It hardly seemed possible that it was over so soon after such a promising start.

"Couldn't come?" Pete said, lowering his *Cottonwood Gazette* to stare at Jeff.

"She has other plans."

"What other plans?" asked Jonathan, who'd just entered the living room. "What could be more important than enduring an evening of the Hardison clan?"

"Would you stop being so damn nosy?" Jeff barked, flopping into a worn leather armchair. "Allison and I aren't joined at the hip."

"Oooookay," Jon said, tiptoeing through the living room toward the kitchen.

Kristin, dressed in a ballet tutu and galoshes, bounced into the room, her face beaming. "Hi, Uncle Jeff!" She climbed into his lap like a puppy. Usually at this point in any visit, she asked him if he'd brought her any treats. He usually managed to stash a roll of Lifesavers or a Hello, Kitty barrette in his pocket for his acquisitive niece whenever he came to visit, but this night he'd forgotten.

It didn't matter, because she wasn't interested in treats. Instead she asked, "Did you bring Allison?"

"No, she couldn't come this time." Because he hadn't asked her. Because he hadn't talked to her in two days, which was probably the longest he and Allison had ever gone without at least talking on the phone.

"Why not?" Kristin asked.

"She had other plans." He hated lying to a little

girl, but he couldn't admit to his family that he and Allison had already broken up. They would all assume it was his fault, and he would never hear the end of it.

Wade, Anne and little Olivia arrived a few minutes later. Anne brought a freshly baked apple pie with her, one of Jeff's favorites. But the mouthwatering smell hardly tempted him tonight. He wasn't much interested in food.

As soon as Anne saw that Jeff was unaccompanied, he had to endure another round of interrogations. The others in his family might be put off by terse excuses, but not Anne.

"Is she doing all right?" Anne asked, sounding overly concerned.

"What do you mean? Of course she's all right. She's just not with me tonight, okay?"

Anne hastily backtracked. "I don't mean anything. I just thought she'd be here. When I talked to her Friday, she planned on being here."

Jeff gave his sister-in-law a sharp look. "If you want to know why she's not here, you can call her and ask."

"Okay, okay, I get the message. Here, you look like you need to hold a baby. Nothing soothes a bad mood like a baby." She thrust Olivia into his arms and turned away to lavish attention on Kristin and Sam.

"Until it's time to change a diaper," Jeff retorted, though he couldn't help but cuddle the baby. She was a cute thing, with her silky red curls and big blue eyes, so trusting.

He intended to have children someday, but he still figured he had plenty of time before he had to settle down.

Allison didn't, he realized. She was thirty-five, edging into those less fertile years. Though lots of women had babies into their forties, many had trouble conceiving as they got older. Maybe it was better that he and Allie had ended their affair. He had no business occupying the last of her fertile years. If she wanted children, she should hook up with a settling-down kind of guy now, before it was too late.

Like the guy in Dallas.

"What is ailing you?" Pete demanded suddenly. "Does that young'un have a dirty diaper?"

"What?"

"You had a look on your face like…like I don't know what."

Jeff handed Olivia to Pete. "Don't worry, there's no dirty diaper. Yet." He headed out the front door and walked toward the barn. He'd never had the affinity for horses that his brothers and grandfather shared, but at least horses wouldn't ask him a bunch of nosy questions.

ON MONDAY MORNING, Anne Hardison shepherded a ten-year-old boy through the front door of Allison's dental office. Randy was attending Wade's Fall-Break Rodeo Camp. Because most of the camp kids were from underprivileged backgrounds, Anne made it a habit to find the ones who needed dental attention and drag them to Allison, who generously donated her services.

Randy had a cavity in his molar the size of a Texas oil well.

Jenny Drew, Allison's receptionist, opened her sliding glass window and smiled. "You can bring Randy in now, Anne."

"Will it hurt?" Randy whispered. He'd been putting on a tough act for her all morning, but it was a pretty tough kid who could act brave in the face of a dentist.

"Dr. Allie is the best dentist in Texas," Anne assured him as she ushered him through the door to the treatment room Jenny pointed to. "I can't guarantee it won't hurt a tiny bit, but she has some really good toys to give away when it's all over."

Randy looked dubious, but he didn't balk as Sandra Dickson, Allison's assistant, helped him into the chair. He held very still for his X rays, then chattered nonstop about how he wanted to ride Beefsteak, the friendly little bull Wade kept for when the older kids showed an interest in bull riding.

Anne didn't tell him his chances of riding Beefsteak were nonexistent—this year, anyway.

A few minutes later Allison entered the treatment room, Randy's X rays in hand. Anne started to greet her friend, but was stunned by Allison's appearance. Her face was puffy and without makeup, her hair looked as if she'd slept on it wet, and her clothes were baggy, nondescript and wrinkled.

Obviously, she hadn't given away all of her "fat clothes."

"Hello, Anne," Allison said, her voice subdued. "And this must be Randy. I'm Dr. Allie." She shook Randy's hand. Though she wasn't her usual cheerful self, her easy manner and soft voice immediately put the child at ease.

Anne was anything but at ease. What in the world was wrong? She knew Allison's medical tests hadn't gone well, and that she was scheduled for surgery later this week. But they'd talked last Friday, and Allison had sounded as though she was handling everything well.

As Allison filled Randy's cavity, Anne sat in a corner and shot her concerned looks, but Allison wouldn't meet her gaze.

"All done," Allison said, giving Randy a hand mirror so he could inspect his new filling.

He seemed pleased. "I wasn't afraid, you know."

"No, you were very brave," Allison said, finally finding a smile as she ruffled the little boy's hair. She showed him a box of toys, from which he picked a set of wax vampire teeth.

"Wait for me in the waiting room, please," Anne told him. "I'll be there in a minute."

"Don't start with me," Allison said as she cleaned up and put away her tools. "I can't be glamorous every single damn day."

"Do you have lunch plans?" Anne asked sharply, taking Allison by surprise.

"Well, no."

"You do now. I have to run Randy back to camp, but then I'm coming here and taking you out for barbecue. No arguments."

When Anne returned forty-five minutes later, Allison was waiting for her. She'd wet combed her hair so that the ends softly curled around her face, and she'd put on a touch of mascara and lipstick. But Anne wasn't fooled.

"Spill it," Anne said after they were seated at Three Z Barbecue, where Allison was eating a plain baked potato and a salad. "You didn't ride your bike this morning?"

"It was too cold."

"You're kidding. I saw you ride once last year when it was snowing."

"I overslept, okay?"

"No, it's not okay. You want to explain why you look like death warmed over?"

"Jeff and I broke up."

Anne almost choked on her ham sandwich. "Already? Damn, I knew something was wrong from the way he was acting Sunday."

"He got all upset because I wouldn't tell him what I was doing in Dallas. He actually thought I was cheating on him. The more I think about it, the madder I get. He accuses me of not trusting him because I won't tell him what I was doing, but he obviously doesn't trust me if he thinks I'd cheat on him."

"Allison." Anne laid her hand on her friend's arm. "What else is he supposed to think when he knows you're keeping secrets from him? You already knew Jeff had a jealous streak. He proved that at the fish fry.''

"He should know me better than that," Allison said, moving the greens around in her salad bowl without actually eating any of them.

"And you should trust him. A relationship without trust is doomed, honey, believe me. I know. I almost wrecked everything with Wade because I wouldn't tell him that I'd had a miscarriage." Anne had feared Wade's reaction to the news, so she'd kept putting it off until she was forced to blurt it out. Wade had been so angry he'd stormed out of her house and left town. It hadn't been the news itself but Anne's unwillingness to trust him that had almost blown the relationship.

"I can't tell him," Allison insisted. "I can't put him through…watching me die."

"Whoa, whoa! Who said anything about dying?"

"It's a possibility," Allison said quietly. "I have to face it. You probably don't remember when Leanne Hardison died. I don't think you'd moved here yet. It tore Jeff up to see his mother suffering like that, but he stayed with her as much as he could, to the very end."

"Allison Crane, I am so angry with you! First off, you aren't going to die. Even if you have cancer, and chances are you don't, we have better ways of treating it than when Leanne Hardison died. And second, Jeff is a strong man. You're underestimating him. Yes, life is harsh sometimes, and he's suffered.

But that's part of being human. He would not want you protecting him from unpleasantness like you're doing.''

"He would feel obligated to stay with me," Allison said. "I couldn't stand it, Anne, I just couldn't. Knowing he'd rather be anywhere else. It's the worst thing I can imagine."

"Okay, worst-case scenario. You have cancer. You have radical surgery, chemo and radiation. Your hair falls out. You're dying."

"Oh, thank you."

"You think Jeff won't notice? And how will that make him feel? Forget about the fact you're sleeping with him. You're his best friend. He'll be by your side, no matter how hard you try to push him away. Whether you're romantically involved or not, you've got twenty-plus years of friendship that can't be tossed out the window.

"He'll be by your side. But he'll never forget the fact you didn't trust him. And that will hurt him more than having to watch you die. I'm sorry for speaking so bluntly, Allie, but I won't stand by and let you screw this up."

Chapter Eleven

"Go home," Jeff's father, Ed Hardison, said at six o'clock Monday night. They were in the business office of the medical suite they shared. The patients were gone, the staff had left, and Jeff was obsessively going over patients' records. He'd found it difficult to concentrate today, and he had this nagging fear that he'd overlooked something.

"I just want to check a few more things. Leona Barker—you used to see her, right?"

"Before I made her mad by telling her she had to lose weight."

"Oh. I was going to ask you if she was always so prickly, but I guess that answers that question."

"She comes in every six weeks with a new complaint, and no matter what you tell her, she ignores the advice. She's looking for a magic pill that will cure all her ailments and magically give her a perfect life."

"Wouldn't we all like to have one of those," Jeff said on a sigh as he replaced Mrs. Barker's chart in the file. He opened another file, but Ed pulled it out of his hands.

"You are in no condition to make decisions about your patients right now. Any fool can see you haven't slept in two days."

"I've slept." Maybe three hours last night.

Ed didn't argue, but he looked troubled. "I wasn't going to mention it, but on her way out, Leona Barker said she wanted to switch back to me. You must have really ticked her off. I've *never* seen you offend a patient."

"I told her to quit whining, get off her butt and exercise, and all of her imaginary illnesses would go away."

"Nice."

"I felt guilty, okay? That's why I was going back over her chart. I don't approve of dismissing a patient's complaint as imaginary. With someone like Mrs. Barker, it would be easy to overlook an actual problem."

"I'll go over her chart with you tomorrow, okay?"

Jeff rubbed his eyes. "Okay."

"Is it Allison?"

"Of course it's Allison. Everybody figured it out last night at dinner. Exactly one week after getting together, we broke up."

"Ah. Well, you had to try, I suppose, or you'd have always wondered."

"Yeah." Jeff stood and went to the coat closet to get his jacket. His father was already wearing his.

"Want to go grab a burger or something?" Ed asked tentatively.

"Sure." Just a couple of cranky, incurable bachelors, out on the town.

They turned out all the lights, and Jeff locked the door to their storefront office. When he turned toward the parking lot, he stopped and stared at his car. Allison was sitting on the hood of his Porsche.

"Then again," Ed said with a low chuckle, "I'm not really hungry. Think I'll head on home."

Jeff waved distractedly to his father as he continued to stare at Allison. He couldn't deny that something inside him jumped to life at the sight of her. But he wasn't sure he was ready to talk to her.

However, he didn't really have a choice, unless he wanted to walk home. She was draped over his windshield.

He approached cautiously. She didn't say anything right away. Her compact was parked next to his car. He leaned against it, folded his arms, and waited. He assumed she had something to say to him.

"We need to talk."

"There's nothing to talk about," he said, "if you're not going to be honest with me."

"But that's why I'm here. I'm willing to tell you everything."

Hope sprang to life in Jeff's chest, along with dread. He knew they couldn't continue unless she trusted him with whatever her big secret was. At the same time, did he really want to know? If she was sleeping with some guy in Dallas, did he really want to hear about it?

He unlocked the passenger door and opened it. "Hop in, then."

"I'd rather walk."

She didn't want to be trapped with him in the car, he guessed. Or she had a lot of nervous energy to work off.

"Let's walk, then."

They headed toward a green space behind the shopping center, where a jogging trail meandered beside a creek. As dusk fell, it was deserted except for one old man walking a schnauzer.

Allison shivered.

"Do you want my jacket?" Jeff asked dutifully.

"No, thanks."

They maintained an uncomfortable silence as they plodded along the path past the old man and dog. Jeff stole a glance at Allison when he could, and was troubled by the shadows under her eyes and her pallid complexion. It seemed she hadn't gotten any more sleep than he had. The combination of fear and vulnerability on her face made his heart ache.

He wanted to stay mad at her. She'd lied to him, and that wasn't something he could just blithely overlook merely because she was having an attack of conscience now.

"You said you wanted to talk," he said, trying to sound dispassionate, all the while rehearsing how he would react when she told him she had another lover. It shouldn't matter so much. They hadn't invested that much in their own romance. It shouldn't be any trouble to just admit that things weren't working and go back to being friends.

"I have a lump in my breast."

What? What had she just said? A buzz started somewhere in the back of Jeff's head.

"You felt it, that first time we made love at the hotel. I told you then it was nothing, but I was lying. I've been going to Dallas for medical tests. Last Thursday was a needle biopsy."

Jeff stopped in his tracks. His brain became so filled with images and information, everything he knew about tumors and biopsies, that he could no longer direct his feet to move, one in front of the other.

A host of medical questions whirled in Jeff's mind. The doctor in him fought for control. He wanted to know what tests she'd had performed and the outcomes. He wanted to see her film, talk with her surgeon, pore over her blood work.

One question finally came to the forefront. "Was it…is it malignant?"

"I don't know yet. The test results are ambiguous."

Ambiguous? What the hell did that mean? Though there was fresh air all around him, Jeff suddenly found it hard to breathe. His lungs felt as if they were shrinking, and his throat had closed to the size of a drinking straw.

Cancer. Allison couldn't possibly have cancer.

The word caused a barrage of horrible images to

whirl through his imagination, memories he'd blocked out for years. His mother's ravaged body, her yellow skin...the fine down on a scalp that used to be covered with thick, blond hair...the moans of pain when even morphine wasn't enough...the smell of her sick room...the sickly strains of organ music at her funeral.

It was too much. Jeff knew he was about to have a meltdown, and that was something Allison didn't need to witness. Didn't she have enough to worry about?

Abruptly he turned and sprinted down the jogging path in the direction they'd come, toward his car. All he could think of was escape. But by the time he reached the parking lot, he knew he hadn't run far enough, so he just kept running, even after his clothes beneath his jacket were soaked with sweat. If he stopped running, he was afraid he would stop breathing and the fear would catch up with him.

He didn't know how much time had passed, but finally his body gave out. He collapsed onto a fallen log near the creek and gasped for air. Gradually his breathing returned to normal.

He knew his reaction wasn't normal. He didn't even know that Allison had breast cancer, only that it was a possibility. But the shock of her news, when he'd been expecting such a completely different type of confession, had felt like a baseball bat to his head.

Why had she kept this secret from him? From him, of all people? Not only was he her lover and her best friend, he was a doctor! Didn't she know why he'd chosen the medical profession? It certainly wasn't for the money. Though he was financially comfortable, he could have done much better practicing in a big city. But he'd chosen to join his father's practice because he was committed to helping the people in Cottonwood and other small towns around here.

People like his mother. People like Allison.

But she hadn't given him the chance to help. Her lack of trust in him was almost as painful as the news of her medical problem.

He shut down that line of thinking. What Allison needed most right now was his support and friendship, not his recriminations. He shuddered to think about the pain he'd caused her with his self-righteous judgments, his accusations of infidelity, his hard-line insistence that she tell him the truth and, finally, his walking out.

He'd just made things worse by running out on her. But she didn't need to witness his weakness. She didn't need to focus on *his* pain.

Jeff stood on shaky legs and started back toward the office, wondering how far he'd run. He needed to pull himself together, then find Allison and apologize for his behavior. He wanted to be there for her. He could get answers from doctors that she might not be able to. He could interpret those damned "ambiguous" tests, or find an expert who could. He could hold her when she was scared.

Or could he? Could he really be a source of strength for her when he was scared to death himself? If the worst came to pass, could he watch her lose her vitality?

Could he watch her fight for her life? Could he watch her die?

ALLISON STOOD for uncounted minutes on the jogging path, watching Jeff run away from his demons—from her. Damn it, she'd known this would happen. She'd been right not to tell him before, and she wished like hell he hadn't pushed her into spilling the news now, before she was ready.

She couldn't deny that, in the back of her mind, she'd held on to the fantasy that Jeff's reaction would be very different. Late last night, as she'd fought for even an hour of sleep, she'd tried to calm herself by envisioning this encounter down to the last detail.

She'd imagined Jeff accepting her news with the quiet confidence that everything would turn out okay. She'd imagined him folding her into his arms and telling her she was worried over nothing. She'd wanted him to tell her about the countless cancer scares he'd dealt with among his patients and how they almost never bore fruit.

Most of all she'd wanted him to assure her that he would be there for her every minute, that he would never turn his back on her no matter what. That he was her friend and lover, and he intended to remain so.

She'd wanted him to tell her he loved her, even if it was a lie. Anything to get her through this.

She sighed as she forced her wooden legs to walk her back to the office parking lot. She might have hoped for a lot of things, but she should have expected what she got. Given Jeff's points of reference, a girlfriend with cancer had to be his worst nightmare.

Jeff's Porsche was still in the parking lot when she got there. That was strange. She'd expected him to be long gone. She thought maybe he'd returned to his office, but it looked dark inside. There was no sign of him anywhere.

Feeling slightly uneasy but not knowing what else to do, Allison climbed into her car and drove herself home.

A message was waiting for her on her answering machine when she walked through the kitchen door. Her hopes skyrocketed, and she chided herself for her disappointment when she pushed the button and heard Anne's voice.

"Call me the minute you get home. Unless you're…busy."

Don't I wish, Allison thought as she erased the message, then went to the stove to put on water for tea. Since Anne was the one who had urged her to make her confession to Jeff, she was naturally interested in the results. Allison supposed she ought to call her friend and tell her the mission had been a total failure. The only good thing was, she'd gotten the lie off her chest. She no longer had to feel guilty about deceiving Jeff.

After she'd brewed her tea, she called Anne.

"So, how'd he do?" Anne asked without preamble.

"He flunked. Miserably. The news freaked him out so badly he ran."

"Ran? What do you mean?"

"I mean he literally ran, turned tail and sprinted for the hills."

"That son of a—"

"Anne, no. Don't say it. It's not his fault. He watched his mother die a slow, painful death, and it had a tremendous impact on him. I don't blame him for running as far and as fast as he can."

"Well, I do! How could he be so insensitive, the heel?"

"It doesn't matter. I know where I stand now, and that's the important thing. If Jeff can't handle even the possibility of illness, then I can't count on him. I need people around me I can rely on. The best thing is to forgive him and move on."

Brave words from someone who felt as if her insides had been put through a food processor.

"Forgive him, my aunt Fanny! He doesn't need forgiveness, he needs a swift kick in the butt!"

"Anne, promise me you'll drop it."

"I'll promise no such thing. Go to bed, Allison. I'm going to fix this for you."

Oh, great. Allison wished she *could* just go to bed. But it was only seven-thirty, and she hadn't eaten dinner. She needed to keep her strength up for the surgery. So she forced herself to thaw a pork chop and some leftover broccoli-rice casserole and down it.

No matter what Anne did, she could not make it right. She might lecture Jeff, or she might threaten to have him tarred and feathered, but it wouldn't matter. Even if he came crawling back to Allison, begging forgiveness, begging for her to let him help her through this crisis, she wouldn't accept it.

He'd made his feelings crystal clear. He might force himself to be with her, to do the right and honorable thing, but all the while he'd be wishing he was elsewhere.

And that she couldn't tolerate.

OTHER MEN TRIED to drink away their troubles; Jeff tried to drown them in ice cream. He soon discovered, though, that the answer to his dilemma could not be found in the bottom of a quart of Ben & Jerry's.

Thirty minutes in his hot tub, sweating out toxins and soothing muscles sure to be sore after his strenuous running, did not bring him any closer to an answer.

He was still parboiling himself when the doorbell rang at about nine that night. He briefly considered that it might be Allison and hoped it wasn't. He wasn't ready to face her yet, not until he figured out what to do.

When he looked through the peephole and saw his sister-in-law standing on his porch, he felt a sense of dread wash over him. Maybe if he was very quiet, and tiptoed away from the door—

"I know you're in there, you worm. Open the door this instant!"

Knowing that if he didn't let her in he would only be postponing the inevitable, not to mention ostracism by his entire family, he released the dead bolt and opened the door.

The moment he did, Anne hurled her leather purse into his stomach with the force of a major-league fast ball. "How could you do it? How could you *do* that to Allison?"

Jeff stepped back, blocking a second blow with his forearm. "Jeez, Anne, settle down!"

"You're just lucky I don't have a gun. What were you thinking? What kind of lowlife scum runs away like a scared rabbit when his lifelong friend tells him she might be sick?"

"A real confused, angry, scared lowlife scum," he shot back. "I'm not exactly proud of running from her, but I had to get out of there or I would have yelled at her."

"For what?" Anne's anger simmered just below the surface.

Jeff prepared himself for another assault, which might come at any time. "For not telling me. For not trusting me to help her. God, Anne, I'm a doctor. I've dedicated my life to healing, yet she wouldn't give me the opportunity to help her."

As Anne continued to stare at him, a cold blast of wind whooshed through his front door.

"You want to come in?" he finally asked, shivering.

She stepped into the foyer, looking him up and down. "Where are your clothes?"

He realized he was wearing only a towel around his hips, and he was dripping on the tile floor. "I was in the hot tub." And he was shivering now as a brisk October breeze whisked into his house.

"Go put a robe on or something."

In his bedroom he dried off and put on sweats,

wishing he had some answers for the questions Anne was bound to ask him. Her father had been one of the finest criminal defense attorneys in Texas before his retirement, and Milton Chatsworth's only child had inherited his talent for interrogation.

When he came back downstairs, he found Anne in his kitchen helping herself to a piece of pie from his refrigerator—a peach pie Allison had baked for him. He started to tell her to put it back, that he wanted the whole thing for himself. It might, after all, be the last pie Allison ever baked for him.

Then he realized how close to the edge he was and kept his mouth shut.

"Couldn't you have just told her you were angry?" Anne said without preamble as she sat down at the table in his breakfast nook with her microwaved pie.

"I couldn't even speak. I wasn't thinking, I just reacted."

"All right, I can understand that," Anne conceded. "But you've had a little time to recover. What's stopping you from calling her now?"

The answer to that question wasn't an easy one. He'd considered calling Allison, had even picked up the phone a couple of times. But every time he even thought about talking to her, his throat started closing up.

"I'm not ready to talk yet."

"Oh, well, pardon me for pushing you out of your comfort zone, but your best friend is sitting home crying because she thinks you don't care about her."

"She knows I care."

"Does she? That's not what you've shown her.

First you wouldn't trust her when she tried to keep something private from you. You accused her of cheating on you, then you bullied her into telling you, when she wasn't ready. Then, instead of facing your own mistake, instead of apologizing for behaving like a cretin, you bolt.''

Anne grabbed his arm, the pie all but forgotten.

"Allison thinks you ran because you aren't willing to suffer any pain on her behalf. She thinks you can't be bothered. What's worse, she believes you're justified. She thinks you went through enough pain when your mother died, and that you shouldn't have to live through it again.''

"That's not it at all.''

"Then go explain to her what it is.''

The thought of Allison crying because of him tore at his gut. Clearly he had to do something. He had to let her know that of course he cared about her. And maybe his ego took a beating because she didn't confide in him at the first sign of trouble. But obviously she'd felt she couldn't trust him that far.

And maybe she was right. Suddenly the truth stared him in the face. "I'm afraid I won't be strong enough for her," he murmured. "I'll crumble when she needs me most.''

Even now, moisture gathered behind his eyes. He hadn't cried in years, not since his mother had died. Out of his whole family, he'd been the only one to cry at his mom's funeral. He'd felt humiliated that he hadn't been able to contain his emotions better. At seventeen he should have had more control. Even Wade, who was only twelve at the time, had remained dry-eyed.

He still remembered the stern looks his grandfather had given him and, even worse, the look of pity and commiseration from his father. Ed had lost his wife, the love of his life, and here he was worrying about a grief-stricken son.

Jeff hadn't cried since, and he sure as hell didn't want to start now.

Anne just shook her head. "I don't understand you at all, Jeff. You waste your life chasing after all these shallow women when you've got Allison right there, like a...like a pearl in an oyster, just waiting to be discovered. And you finally come to your senses and find your way to her...

"Now, a week later, you're going to lose her."

ANNE'S WORDS STAYED with Jeff a long time, returning to the forefront of his mind at odd times to haunt him. He wasn't going to lose Allison—he'd already lost her. He'd done everything wrong, said everything wrong. And if by some miracle he managed to win her over, to convince her he was worthy of a second chance?

He might lose her again.

After yet another sleepless night and the longest morning in history, during which every single patient got on his nerves, he decided having Allison hate him for being a gutless wimp was worse than a ticket to hell. For God's sake, how could he worry about his own possible losses, especially a loss of pride, at a time like this?

So what if he broke down in front of her, became a blubbering fool. At least she would know he cared.

Noon couldn't come soon enough. The moment

he finished with his last morning patient, he took off his lab coat, grabbed his jacket and headed out of the office without a word of explanation to anyone. Ten minutes later he was pulling up in front of Allison's office, hoping to catch her before she left for her own lunch.

"You just missed her," Jenny, the receptionist, informed him.

"Where'd she go?"

"I'm not supposed to give out that information to—"

"For crying out loud, Jenny, it's me. Just tell me where she went for lunch."

Jenny sighed. "The Grapevine. Don't tell her I told."

The Grapevine was a frou-frou tearoom located in the antique mall on the square. Jeff had never set foot in it—few men had. It featured dishes like tiny crustless sandwiches, fruit salad cups and spinach quiche, along with fruit-flavored iced tea. The decor had enough ruffles and cabbage roses to gag Laura Ashley.

All of that didn't stop Jeff from strolling through the front door of the mall and into the tearoom, bold as you please, in search of his quarry.

At first all he saw was a sea of blue hair. But then he saw a flash of red. He should have known Allison would be lunching with Anne, the two of them probably commiserating on what a snake he was.

His courage faltered as a collective gasp went up when the lunching ladies saw him, but only for a moment. He strode past the gingham-clad hostess straight to Anne and Allison's table. He pulled out one of the extra chairs and sat down as the two women gaped at him.

"Thanks for saving me a place," he said as a woman with a perennial sneer on her face handed him a menu and set a glass of water in front of him. "So, what's good here?"

"Jeff, what are you doing here?" Allison finally asked. "And don't tell me you've suddenly developed an interest in growing orchids."

"What?"

Anne could hardly contain her mirth. "You just crashed a meeting of the Cottonwood Gardening Society."

Chapter Twelve

Jeff was suddenly aware of a couple of dozen pairs of sharp eyes assessing him, wondering what he was doing in this bastion of female flower nurturers—and wondering what would happen next. He held his ground. This was important. He had to get through to Allison, even if it meant enduring a little discomfort.

"You know, I'm not really very hungry," Anne said. "Jeff, you can have my shrimp salad. I haven't even touched it yet. I'll go sit at my mother's table." She beat a hasty retreat.

Allison just stared at him as she took a bite of her pasta salad. The whole serving could have fitted in a one-cup measure.

"You want to go somewhere else?" he asked.

"I'm sure whatever you have to say to me, you can say here." She was trying to be cold and impassive, but she didn't succeed. Instead, she came off as hurt and vulnerable, which almost did Jeff in. His throat started tightening, but he didn't let it. He gulped down half a glass of water. The tightness in his throat eased.

"Where do I start?" he asked, though he didn't expect an answer. "An apology, maybe, though I can't imagine anything I could say that would convince you how sorry I am."

"Sorry for what? For wanting to avoid pain?"

"For panicking. That's what it was, pure and simple."

"I dumped the news on you without preparing you first. It's okay."

"Of course it's not okay. You're my best friend. I should have been strong for you. I should have offered you encouragement and comfort and hope."

"And I should have trusted you from the beginning. You were right about that. The fact that we'd gotten involved...physically..." Her carefully chosen words tiptoed around their relationship. "It muddled my thinking. Everything was so perfect, and I didn't want to spoil that."

"It was perfect," he agreed. "It still can be."

"No."

The single word was like a knife to Jeff's heart. "Why not?"

"Because these last few days have been the most painful of my life," she said matter-of-factly. "When I told you I could handle it, if and when you decided to end our relationship, I was lying through my teeth. I was devastated after you walked out. I wanted to crawl under a rock and never come out. Needless to say, such feelings aren't conducive to healing. *Healing* may be the operative word in my life in the months to come.''

''I can help.''

Allison shook her head. ''If the news is bad, you wouldn't want to stick around for the long haul.''

''Of course I would.''

''No, Jeff. Because you always have to be the one to leave.''

''What are you talking about?''

''The dating and mating habits of Jeff Hardison have been of prime interest to me for quite some time. You start out by falling for women without a lot of substance to them. Then, at the first sign of trouble, you deliver the let's-just-be-friends speech and move on. You can't stand the idea of being the one left behind.

''Well, not to be the voice of gloom and doom,'' she continued, ''but I might just be the one to leave. Not by my choice, but still... And I don't think you could handle it. I don't believe you'd stay with me over the long haul.''

Her eyes shimmered with tears. If she started crying, he'd be a goner. ''Don't you dare cry,'' he said. ''If you do, the old biddies who are watching our every move will know it's my fault, and they'll ride me out of town on a rail.''

She managed a halfhearted laugh, then took a long drink of water.

''Allison, I won't leave you,'' he said, determined to convince her. ''I won't pretend I'm not horrified at the thought of anything bad happening to you. I can't guarantee I'll always be a pillar of strength for you. But I'll be here. On call, anytime you want me or need me.''

She reached over and put her hand on his. ''Thank you, Jeff. I know how hard this is for you, and I appreciate your trying to do the right thing.''

Frustration welled up inside of him. ''You think I'm just saying all this out of guilt? Or because Anne made me do it?''

''I wouldn't want Anne mad at *me*.''

''Anne did pay me a visit. I won't deny she used her…special brand of persuasion on me. Maybe she brought me to my senses a little sooner than I would have come to them on my own, but let's get one thing straight. I'm here because I want to be here.''

Allison seemed to be thinking about his words. She buttered a roll, then put it down without eating it.

Finally she spoke. ''Why don't we talk about this again…later?''

''Later, when?''

''After my surgery.''

''*What* surgery?''

''A lumpectomy. It's not a big deal, not yet.''

Jeff had to consciously quell his panic. ''When?''

''Soon.''

''When?'' he asked again. ''I want to be there.''

''No.''

''So you don't want to talk about this until you know for sure, one way or another.''

''Exactly.'' She seemed pleased that he understood. "If I get a clean bill of health, we can start again and forget this ever happened."

Jeff let himself fantasize about that for a moment. His fondest wish was for this cancer scare to go away, and he could be with Allison again without this horrible threat standing between them. But he could not let himself feel joyful at the prospect, because he had to think about the alternative.

"And if things go the other way? If you get bad news?"

She shrugged. "I would never expect you to want me then."

The hurt lurking behind those words was almost Jeff's undoing. Again, he felt the pressure in his throat, this time accompanied by a painful squeezing of his heart. And he knew that what he said now in response to her pain would set the tone for everything that would follow.

"Allie, I'll still want you, no matter what."

"Even if I elect to have radical surgery?"

Jeff had come to appreciate Allison's beautiful, round breasts the way a starving man appreciates bread. It was horrible to think about one of them disappearing. But his feelings for Allison ran far deeper than those surface things he loved about her. "Yes," he answered with certainty.

"Even if I end up dying? It won't be pretty. It never is."

"I know that as well as anyone. Yes, even if..."

"You can't even say the words."

Because he was superstitious about saying it.

Speaking aloud the worst possibility might make it come true.

"Jeff, I know you're trying. But I would never tie you to me. If I have cancer, you just go on your merry way. Promise me."

"In a pig's eye."

"Promise me. Or so help me I'll burst into the noisiest, messiest tears you ever saw, and the garden club ladies won't let you out of this tearoom alive."

He shook his head. "Won't work. When is your surgery?"

She paused before answering. "I don't know the exact time. I'll let you know, okay?"

She was lying. If she wanted to exclude him so badly that she would lie to do it, then maybe he should let her. He was walking a fine line between proving he cared about her and causing her stress. And she didn't need the stress.

"All right." He laid a ten-dollar bill on the table, though he'd consumed nothing except water, and walked out with a dozen pairs of beady eyes watching him suspiciously.

ALLISON TRULY BELIEVED she'd done the right thing. She loved Jeff—especially since he'd tried so hard to make up for his earlier behavior. But her assessment of him was accurate. He couldn't bear the thought of being the one left behind, and she would not put him through that.

She would not bind him to her through obligation and guilt.

Anne rejoined her at the table, but she did not launch an interrogation, as was her normal habit. Instead she ordered the most decadent dessert on the menu along with two spoons.

"He did the right thing," Allison finally said when they were halfway through their double-fudge sundae.

"Mmm, hmm." Anne wasn't going to press her.

"You don't have to beat him up anymore. I threw him for a loop with the big *C* word, but he's recovered and he's sorry he reacted badly."

"That's it?"

"Yeah." Allison forced a smile. "Whew, glad that's over."

"But you're not back together."

"No. I don't want to be back together with him."

"You fat liar!"

At the mention of the word *fat*, Allison put aside her spoon, even though she knew Anne wasn't referring to weight. "If everything turns out okay, we might get back together."

"Is that what he said?" Anne was well on the way to building up another good case of outrage.

"No, no, that's what I said."

"So, if you're healthy, you'll reconcile. Until the next crisis. Allison, is that the kind of relationship you want? Fair-weather lovers?"

"No, but I'm afraid that's the only kind of lovers we'll ever be."

"You won't even give him a chance to prove you wrong?"

No. Because if he proved her right, she didn't know if she was strong enough to withstand the pain. "I can't think about this anymore. My surgery is tomorrow. I just want to get through that. And I certainly don't want to use it as some kind of test to see whether Jeff is worthy. Give him a break, Anne. Jeff is Jeff. I'll still feel the same way about him next week as I did last week."

"You really love him, don't you?"

Endlessly. She'd had no idea a broken heart could hurt so much—more even than her years of unrequited love. "Yeah."

"So much that you won't risk finding out whether he really loves you."

Anne was right. And Allison wasn't sure she wanted to know the answer to that question.

JEFF LEFT THE TEAROOM feeling ambivalent about his decision to let Allison get away with her lie. But what could he do about it, besides pester her? He might be able to worm the specifics about her surgery from Anne, or Allison's parents, but what good would that do him? He could show up at the hospital where she was having her operation and hang out in the waiting room, and try to prove to her he could be there for her during tough times. But he would probably just end up irritating her, upsetting her family, feeling like an outsider.

Allison's assessment of his relationship potential had stung, but after only a short reflection, he'd realized she was right. He did always try to leave first.

He had a hard time with long-term commitments of any kind, because the idea of being left alone bothered him.

All he had to do was look at his family to know why. His mother had died, what, eighteen years ago? And his father had been alone all that time, choosing not to find another partner. Jonathan's wife had left him when Kristin was still in diapers, and Jonathan had been bitter and alone ever since. Even his grandmother had left, long before Jeff was born, and old Pete had spent uncounted years as a cranky loner.

With examples like that all around him, how could Jeff believe in happily-ever-after, much less in his own ability to survive if the woman he loved left him, alone and hurting, to fend for himself?

Returning to his office, he braced himself for the inevitable questions. But his receptionist was gone to her own lunch, and the office was all but deserted. Only his father was there, sitting in his office with the door open, munching a sandwich as he opened mail.

Jeff tried to sneak past, but Ed caught sight of him. "Jeff. Have you had lunch?"

He sighed. "Not exactly."

"I've got enough sandwiches here to feed a family of grizzly bears. Mrs. Barker brought over a picnic basket, and she said it was for both of us. I think it's her way of apologizing."

"That was nice," Jeff said blandly, shrugging out of his jacket. Ed pointed to the basket, and Jeff found a pimiento cheese sandwich. He'd have probably done better to eat that shrimp salad at the tea-room. He unwrapped the cellophane from the sandwich and eyed it dubiously, wondering if Mrs. Barker might have laced it with arsenic.

"Is everything…okay?" Ed asked tentatively.

"No. I was just thinking what a dismal track record our family has when it comes to women."

"I used to think the same thing. But lately I've seen signs of hope. Pete has Sally now. And Wade—never saw a man so changed."

"Yeah, but then there's you and me and Jonathan."

"Yeah. Well, caring about someone entails a certain amount of risk. The highs can shoot you into the stratosphere, but the lows…"

"Risking the lows has got to be better than keeping all your feelings under lock and key."

Ed looked up. "Are you talking about me or yourself?"

"I'm afraid I'm purely into self-centeredness right now. I've been living a lot of years just feeling everything on the surface. And I just realized that that's not really living."

"Since when?"

"Since Allison made me fall in love with her. It's the best thing that ever happened to me—and the worst."

"Have you told her?"

Just mentioning the idea threw Jeff into fight-or-flight mode—accelerated heart, tense muscles, adrenaline shooting through his veins.

"I take it that means no," Ed said.

Jeff took a bite of his sandwich and chewed it slowly, then swallowed. "Maybe that's all she's been waiting for—for me to lay it on the line, put my heart on a platter where she can slice and dice it at her leisure."

Instead he'd tiptoed around the word *love*, just as she had done. They had referred to their "relationship." They'd talked about getting "involved physically." He'd said he would "want" her. He'd called her his best friend, he'd said he would "be there," that she could call him.

But he hadn't said he loved her. He hadn't committed to her in the most convincing way a man could commit.

A brilliant idea suddenly caught his fancy. What a wonderful, bold gesture that would be! How could she doubt the constancy of his feelings then? She would go into her surgery with her heart glowing with love.

Suddenly Jeff laid down the sandwich and grabbed his jacket.

"Where are you going?" Ed asked.

"To buy a ring."

Ed's face lit up. "You don't have to *buy* one."

Jeff snapped his fingers. "That's right. Grandma Lawton's ring." He stopped at his dad's office door and turned. "If this works out okay, we're gonna work on you next. Being alone sucks."

Ed just laughed. "You go, son."

JEFF DROVE HOME, even though he could have walked it, but he was too impatient. In his bedroom, he went to the top drawer of his dresser where he kept an odd assortment of things he didn't know what else to do with. There were cuff links, always a popular Christmas present even though he never wore them. A sack of beloved marbles, which he'd been meaning to give to Sam. Some antique coins. But no ring.

Where had he put the damn thing? He checked the top shelf of his closet, under the bed, in his desk drawers. Just when he was about to give up in despair, he found the velvet ring box in the very back of a kitchen cabinet behind the juicer Allison had given him for his birthday one year.

He remembered now, that he'd stuck the ring back there where he'd never see it, because of all the sad memories it evoked.

Before her death, his mother had given each of her sons a piece of her jewelry. She'd given Grandma Lawton's ring to Jeff, and warned him that he'd better find some girl to marry someday, or she would haunt him.

He was actually able to smile now, at the memory. Leanne Hardison had never lost her spirit or her sense of humor, even toward the end of her life. And she'd somehow known that Jeff, out of her three sons, would be the commitment-shy one.

He opened the box and studied the huge oval diamond flanked by smaller stones. It was enough to knock a woman's eye out. And if diamonds alone weren't enough to impress Allison, surely the sentimental value he attached to the ring would make her understand he meant business. At the very least, the ring was tangible evidence that his proposal was premeditated.

He took the ring to a jewelry store to have it cleaned. Then he endured the rest of the afternoon. His last patient left at four. Bursting with optimism and eager to put his plan into action, he headed straight for Allison's office—and found it closed.

That was odd. She was usually open until six on Tuesdays. He tried her house, then peeked through the window in the garage door. Her car and her bike were both in there, but she wasn't home.

He tried her cell phone, but she didn't answer, so he left a message. She hadn't picked up her mail, so he pulled a magazine from her mailbox and sat on her porch swing to wait for her. She had to come home eventually.

After he had read *Cosmo* cover to cover, he knew a lot more about how to drive men crazy in bed— not that he'd want to try—but he still didn't know where Allison was. It was growing dark. Where could she be?

Rather than waiting, he decided to drive around. He tried her parents' house first, but Lester and Barbara weren't home. The house was dark, and even their Chihuahua, Jonas, was silent. He tried some of Allison's favorite restaurants—there weren't that many in Cottonwood—but she wasn't at any of them. Finally he drove to Wade's place, thinking she might have gone to visit Anne.

The bright orange of a fire drew his eye. Alarmed, he drove as close as he could get, then approached on foot toward a clearing in the trees behind the main house.

He soon realized it was just a campfire. About a dozen kids were gathered around it. Jamie Collins, a local storyteller, was playing his guitar and singing one of his trademark songs about the Wild West, and the children were obviously enthralled.

Wade and Sally, who sometimes worked as the camp cooks, were at a nearby picnic table making hamburger patties. There was no trace of Anne or Allison, probably a sign they were together.

"Well, look who's here!" Sally cried out in greeting.

Wade's greeting was more subdued. "Jeff? What are you doing here? Is something wrong?"

"No, something's finally right," Jeff said. "I'm looking for Allison. Is she somewhere with Anne?"

Wade's face, illuminated by the campfire, got a guarded look. "They might be together," he said carefully. Sally got a guilty look on her face and busied herself with the hamburger meat, withdrawing altogether from the conversation.

Jeff immediately went on alert. "C'mon, bro, you know something."

"I do, but I'm sworn to secrecy."

"What is this, junior high? Just tell me."

"I can't."

Jeff had wanted Allison to be the first to know of his intentions, but he had to find some way to unclamp Wade's jaws. He pulled the ring box out of his jacket pocket. "Look. See this? I'm going to propose to her."

"Well, it's about time," Sally said.

"Wow, that's Grandma Lawton's ring." Wade grinned. "Way to go, Jeff. I knew you'd wake up and smell the coffee sooner or later."

"Then you'll tell me where she is?"

That guarded shadow came back over Wade's face. "Can't you propose to her in a couple of days? Or next week? I think it'd be better."

Like a bolt of lightning, Jeff realized where Allison was. "Oh, hell. She's gone to Dallas. She's having her surgery."

Wade didn't deny it.

"Damn it, I wanted to be there with her."

"You probably don't want to throw something at her like a marriage proposal, not right now. She doesn't need the stress."

"But don't you see? If I wait till she's had the surgery, she'll think I only want her because she *doesn't* have cancer. Or if she does—" he knocked on the wooden table "—that I'm asking out of guilt. I have to make her understand that I want her under any circumstances, whether she's fat or skinny, sick or healthy—"

"For richer for poorer, yeah, yeah, I get it."

"Then you'll tell me where she is?"

Wade hesitated.

"Oh, just tell him," Sally said.

After another long pause, Wade finally spoke. "She and Anne drove to Dallas with Allison's parents. They're all staying at Allison's aunt's house, and she has surgery scheduled for first thing tomorrow morning."

"All right, now we're getting somewhere. Which hospital?"

"That, I don't know."

"Then who's the aunt? What's her name?"

Wade shrugged helplessly. "Don't know that, either."

"I don't suppose you know the name of the doctor?"

"Really, I don't. I'd tell you if I did. And before you ask, Anne forgot her cell phone, so I can't reach her that way, either."

Jeff patted Wade's arm. "That's okay. I'll find her." And he would, if he had to comb every hospital in Dallas tomorrow morning.

JEFF WOKE AT FIVE the next morning in his Dallas hotel room. Last night's phone calls to hospitals had been unproductive. Employees were fanatical about patient privacy these days, and no one would tell him whether Allison Crane was scheduled for surgery the next morning.

As he stood in the shower, he decided he'd pull out the big guns. He was friends with the head of thoracic surgery at Baylor Medical Center. That was a doctor whose name opened doors. Ken would find out what Jeff needed to know.

Jeff decided six was late enough. He called Ken's home and got him out of bed.

"If I don't find this woman and propose to her before she has surgery, my life is ruined," Jeff said melodramatically. "Can you pull some strings and find her?"

"Are you nuts? You got me out of bed so you can harass some preoperative woman? Take a Valium, Hardison." *Click.*

Jeff realized that just maybe he'd crossed the line over to insanity, but he didn't care. It felt better to be insane than to feel nothing. He would just have to handle this another way.

He visited the hospitals personally, hitting the larger ones first and working his way down the list. He wore his white coat, which got him attention a helluva lot faster than if he were just a civilian seeking information about a nonblood relative.

His first three visits yielded no results. Fourth on the list was Woodland Memorial. He entered the main lobby, then followed the signs toward the surgery wing, finally arriving at an information desk of some sort. A harried-looking volunteer in a pink uniform was entering some information in the computer.

"Excuse me, ma'am," Jeff said in his most befuddled voice, "I'm Dr. Jeff Hardison. I'm assisting on a surgery for an Allison Crane, and I need to know which room."

The volunteer smiled up at him and batted her eyelashes. Then she punched a few buttons on her machine. "Ms. Crane's surgery is in room four, in the Day Surgery Center across the street. She should be in preop, now."

Pay dirt! The AMA would probably yank his license if they knew he was posing as a surgeon, but "desperate times" and all that. He smiled his thanks at the volunteer and took off out the front doors and across the street.

A friendly nurse pointed him toward Allison's cubicle, where she was being prepped for surgery. Another nurse was exiting the cubicle as Jeff approached, drawing the curtain.

This one was less friendly. She gave Jeff a critical once-over, not impressed by his white coat. "Can I help you?"

"I'm Dr. Hardison, Ms. Crane's physician from back home. I'm also a...family friend. I just came to wish her luck."

The nurse frowned and checked Allison's chart, which was in a pocket outside the door. "Oh, yes, there you are, Ed Hardison. You're not really supposed to be back here."

"I just want a minute with her." He gave the woman his most winning smile.

"All right. But she's just been given Demerol, so she might be a little groggy."

Jeff entered the cubicle. Allison was on a gurney with a sheet draped over her. Only her head, shoulders and one arm were visible. Her hair was tucked into a sterile cap, and she was connected to an IV. Her face had been scrubbed free of makeup.

She'd never looked so beautiful to him, her face serene, like an angel. Her eyes were closed.

"Allison?"

Her eyelids fluttered, then opened. She struggled to focus. "Jeff?"

He took her hand. "I'm here for you, darling. Allison, I've been so stupid. I love you. I want to marry you." He pulled the ring box out of his coat pocket and opened it for her, holding it in front of her face.

"Will you marry me, Allison?"

"'S pretty," she said with a stuporous smile. "Can I have some ice cream, now?"

"No, Allie, listen. It's me, Jeff." But she'd closed her eyes again.

"Mama said I could have ice cream."

"Yes, I'll give you ice cream. Anything you want. If you'll marry me." Jeff realized how futile his efforts were. She was fast falling deeper under the drug's influence. He couldn't expect her to make a lifetime commitment under these circumstances.

He caressed her face. "Be safe. I'll be waiting for you. I love you."

"Love you...too..." She started snoring.

Jeff slipped the diamond ring onto her finger. She hadn't said yes, but he wanted her to see the ring first thing when she woke up.

Chapter Thirteen

Allison drifted on the softest cloud imaginable. While floating there in perfect comfort, she saw Jeff's face suspended in the air over her.

"I love you," he said in the most adoring voice.

"I love you, too," she said back. Then she saw a star that was brighter than the sun. It blinded her for a second. After that, she and Jeff were walking down this path strewn with gold dust, holding hands, enveloped in a cloud of pure bliss.

Gradually she became aware of a fly in the ointment of her perfect dream. Pain, and a lot of it. Needles in her arm, and a horrible ache in the area of her left breast.

She started crying. Jeff was gone, and she was in this horrible black void. "Oh, Jeff, why couldn't it be real?" she sobbed.

"She's coming out."

Who was that? Allison continued to sob, not really sure why. She realized she could come out of the black void if she would just open her eyes. But when she did, horrible bright lights hit her in the face.

She'd had her tonsils out, and she was coming out of surgery. Then why did her chest hurt?

Then she remembered. She forced herself to open her eyes and look down. They were both still there! Thank God. Before surgery, she'd signed a bunch of forms. One of them had given her surgeon permission to perform radical surgery if her tumor turned out to be cancer.

Did this mean she was okay, that the tumor was benign?

She opened her eyes all the way and looked up. Her surgeon, Dr. Evans, was there smiling at her.

"I wanted to be the first to tell you. You're clean, no trace of cancer in the preliminary lab report. Your only souvenir of today will be a few stitches and a little scar."

"Th-th—" Apparently her tongue hadn't yet awakened from the anesthetic.

"You're welcome," Dr. Evans said before leaving her recovery room.

"Good news, huh?" said the nurse who was monitoring Allison's recovery. "Makes my job more fun. How are you feeling?"

Allison marshaled all her resources to get her mouth to cooperate. "Crappy," she managed. "No, I'm on top of the world. No cancer. No cancer!" She giggled almost hysterically, then stopped abruptly. "But I still feel like tossing my cookies."

The nurse laughed. "You'll feel better in a while."

JEFF HAD NOT MET with a welcoming committee in the Day Surgery waiting room. After Allison's parents and Anne got over the shock of seeing him there, they pelted him with questions and recriminations.

"What are you doing here?"

"How did you find Allison?"

"You'd better not upset her."

Jeff held up his hands, warding off the verbal attack. "Whoa, wait a minute. I'm here because I care about Allison. I found her by driving around Dallas like a nutcase, visiting every hospital I passed until I found the right one. And I have no intention of upsetting her."

"Couldn't you wait?" Barbara Crane asked gently. "Visit her after she's back on her feet? She won't want you to see her when she's not looking or feeling her best."

"It won't make any difference to me," Jeff insisted. He started to explain that he loved her, that he would take her no matter what shape she was in. But at the last moment he decided he should work things out with Allison before making any more public declarations.

Mr. Crane said nothing, just glared at Jeff with his protruding eyes. Jeff remembered that look from when he was a kid. The Reverend Lester Crane had glared at his congregation from the pulpit with that same expression of disapproval whenever he was talking about sin, which he did during most sermons.

After an interminable amount of time, a doctor in scrubs entered the waiting room. He went to where the Cranes and Anne were sitting, excluding Jeff. Of course, he didn't know Jeff was waiting on news about Allison.

Jeff eavesdropped shamelessly.

"She came through the surgery beautifully. We sent the tumor to the lab, and by all indications, it's benign."

Barbara Crane sagged against her husband with relief, and Anne hugged them both.

"She's in recovery now, just waking up. Someone will take you back to see her in a few minutes." The doctor strode back toward the O.R.

Jeff closed his eyes and savored the news. She was okay. Allison was going to live. The relief was like a sweet, hot fire bursting to life in his chest, radiating outward into every pore of his skin. She would live for another sixty or seventy years, if he had anything to say about it. She would marry him, and they would have beautiful children together.

Slowly he came to realize Anne was sitting beside him. "You okay?" she asked.

He smiled. "Fine. Great." He blinked back the moisture in his eyes. "I want to see her. Anne, you were right about everything. I've behaved like a total ass, but I'm going to make everything right, I promise."

"Her parents want to see her first. They said they would tell her you're here."

"Okay. I'll wait, but I'm not waiting long."

After a few more minutes a nurse came to get the

Cranes, and they went to recovery to visit their daughter. A few minutes more, and the same nurse called for Anne to come back.

Jeff waited alone, wondering what was taking so long. He was ready to barge into recovery without invitation when Anne reappeared, her expression so solemn it alarmed him.

"Is she okay?" he asked.

"She's fine. But, Jeff, she doesn't want to see you."

The news hit him like a freezing waterfall. "Why...why not?"

Allison shrugged. "She just said no. In all fairness, she's still very groggy, and she's not thinking straight. Maybe she just doesn't want you to see her when she's not at her best."

"She's always at her best," Jeff murmured.

Anne patted his arm. "Give her a day or two. One trauma at a time."

He didn't want to be a trauma to her.

"Tell her to please call me when she's feeling better, okay."

"I will."

Jeff left the hospital, completely deflated. It was ironic that he'd finally figured out what was in his heart, a day too late.

ALLISON STILL FELT lethargic, but at least she could stand up. It had taken her fifteen minutes to put her clothes back on, and another ten to tie her shoes.

She felt as if she had seven or eight thumbs on each hand.

But at least she was going home, or rather, to her aunt Betsy's house. Aunt Betsy would ply her with homemade soup and pot roast and fresh-baked cherry cobbler, and for once Allison wouldn't worry about her fat grams. She intended to indulge herself and wallow in her relief over the good news.

A nurse came into her cubicle carrying a manila envelope. "Dr. Evans will be here shortly to release you. Here's your jewelry."

Allison didn't take the envelope. "That's not mine."

"It's got your name on it."

"I took all my jewelry off before coming to the hospital." She'd heard horror stories about valuables disappearing during surgery.

"Are you sure?" The nurse opened the sealed envelope and reached inside. "Wow."

Allison examined the ring the nurse held up to the light. It was a stunning, oval-shaped diamond surrounded by smaller diamonds, all set in what appeared to be platinum. Obviously an antique, it flashed and winked like the sun. "Wow is right. I wish it *were* mine. But I've never seen it before."

"Hmm. Well, I'm sure it belongs to someone. I'll just listen for the anguished screams from whatever woman is missing her engagement ring."

Allison thanked the nurse, then sat in a chair to wait for the doctor to release her. After about five minutes he obliged her. Her parents and Anne came to collect her, and she left the hospital, hoping she wouldn't ever have to see the inside of it again.

"Can I tell Jeff something?" Anne asked her as they walked toward the parking lot. "Anything?"

"I need some time, that's all."

"That's a pretty small crumb, but I guess it'll have to do."

JEFF WAITED. And waited. He didn't want to crowd Allison. She'd asked for time, through Anne, which gave him a sliver of hope. At least she hadn't told him to jump off the nearest bridge.

Sooner or later she would have to talk to him. She had his ring, after all. The fact she hadn't returned it was further evidence that she wasn't going to reject him. He just had to be patient.

Unfortunately, sooner came sooner than he expected, and in a most unwelcome way.

It was a cold, dreary Saturday afternoon just after Halloween. Jeff had gone to the Hardison Ranch to help celebrate Kristin's seventh birthday. After cake and ice cream and mountains of Barbie paraphernalia, Kristin declared that her birthday wouldn't be complete unless she went to see the new Pony Princess movie, which had just opened at the Cottonwood Cineplex.

"I think we should all go," Anne declared. The men all grumbled at her suggestion, but Sam's protest was more strident.

"I am *not* going to see any movie that has anything to do with ponies and princesses," he declared. "If any of my friends saw me, I'd be doomed."

Pete, Ed and Wade also managed to make up excuses for skipping this outing, but Jeff wasn't fast enough.

"C'mon, Jeff." Jonathan punched his brother in the arm. "Ponies in ballet tutus. What could be more fun? And," he added under his breath, "I refuse to be the only adult male in the theater."

"C'mon, Uncle Jeff," Kristin pleaded. "Please? Please, please, please?"

Jeff caved. He consoled himself by believing this would be good practice for when he and Allison had their own children.

As soon as Kristin was settled in with her Juju Fruits, Jeff put the earphone from his portable radio into his ear and tuned into a football game—the Texas Longhorns vs. the Oklahoma Sooners. Sometimes the announcer's description of the game matched the tutu-wearing ponies' antics in comical ways, and Jeff laughed at inappropriate times, earning censorious stares from Kristin.

"Uncle Jeff, want some Juju Fruits?" Kristin whispered.

"No, thank you." Not after all that cake and ice cream.

"But I don't like the black ones."

"Then don't eat them. No, no, don't drop them on the floor. Kristin!"

"But I'm afraid I'll accidentally eat one."

Jeff sighed. "Give them to me."

This proved to be a near-fatal mistake. During a particularly tense fourth-and-goal, Jeff absently popped one of the black Juju's into his mouth and chewed. Moments later he felt a stabbing pain in the back of his mouth. A bit of panicked exploring with his tongue revealed that the sticky candy had broken one of his molars. It was the tooth that had been hurting, the one Allison had suggested he let her X-ray, only he'd ignored her advice.

Now he was paying for it.

"Back in a minute," he whispered to Kristin, only it sounded more like "Bag idda muhnuh." He went to the rest room, where he rinsed his mouth out with warm water and examined the tooth. It wasn't a pretty sight, and it hurt like hell.

Damn it, he would have to make an emergency visit to a dentist. And the only dentist he knew was Allison.

He returned to the pony movie and found Jonathan, whispering that he needed to go home and he would take a cab.

Jon slid out of his chair, and the two of them went into the lobby. "You're doing what?"

"I broke a tooth on a Juju Fruit," Jeff explained. He could feel sweat popping out on his forehead, though the theater complex was quite cool. "You don't happen to know the name of a dentist other than Allison, do you?"

Jonathan grinned. "Are you crazy? You've been

looking for an excuse to see her for days. She can't turn you down, you're in pain.''

"Hey, you may be right."

"Good luck. Let me know how it goes." Jonathan turned back toward the theater.

"You seem awful anxious to get back to the ponies," Jeff called after him.

"The evil Palomino Queen has just banished poor Princess Buffy to the volcano cave, where ponies go in, but they don't come out."

Jeff felt the same way about dentistry as Princess Buffy probably felt about the volcano cave. But he knew Allison wouldn't deliberately hurt him, no matter what her personal feelings for him were. He called for the cab, then dialed her office number. Her answering service took the call and said they would page her.

Ten minutes later Allison called Jeff's cell phone.

"Jeff, are you okay?"

Her concern warmed him. "Broke a tooth."

"The one that was hurting?"

"Yes, and I don't need to hear 'I told you so.' I just need you to put me out of my misery."

"Hurts, huh?"

"Well, you don't need to gloat."

"Jeff, I would never gloat about pain. Can you meet me at my office in about twenty minutes?"

"Yes. Allison?"

"What?"

"Are you up to this? Have you recovered from your surgery?"

"I'm fine. Thank you for asking." She hung up, leaving Jeff with a sense of foreboding about the coming meeting. She didn't want to see him. He could hear it in her voice.

ALLISON KNEW she had to get through the next few minutes somehow. She wasn't ready to see Jeff. She'd just gotten back from a bike ride, eight miles of drizzle, and she was wilted and windblown. There was no time to primp. Poor Jeff was hurting, and she couldn't in good conscience make him wait while she fixed her hair and put on lipstick.

She peeled off her damp clothes, threw on jeans and a sweatshirt and headed for her office.

Jeff was waiting for her by the door, and he was wearing those jeans she loved, the faded-almost-white ones that hugged his rear so appealingly. *Why those jeans?* But she forced her mind out of the gutter when she realized Jeff was truly in pain. She could tell just by the way he was standing, one hand cupping his face.

This wasn't some ruse to see her, she realized, her heart going out to him.

"How did this happen?" she asked as soon as she climbed out of her car.

"Candy. I was at the movies with Kristin and Jon. I'm not sure which is worse—a broken tooth, or another hour of angst over Buffy the Princess Pony."

She unlocked the door and let them both inside. "Oh, right. Kristin's birthday." She'd been invited to Kristin's party. But she hadn't been up to facing Jeff, so she'd begged off, thinking she would drop off her present for Kristin at the ranch later today—after Jeff had gone home.

Allison led Jeff into one of her treatment rooms and put him in the chair. He looked especially inviting, stretched out like that, and it took all of her willpower not to touch him. She'd be touching him enough during the actual dental work, and that would be difficult enough.

"I'll have to do this without an assistant," she said, "so it'll be slow going."

"Great. Painful *and* slow."

"Now, you know I'm painless." She washed her hands, taking an extra long time, delaying the moment at which she would have to get close to him.

"I don't know any such thing," he grumbled. "I've never even had a cavity."

"Well, there's nothing to it." She turned toward him, bracing herself as she positioned the overhead lamp. "Open up and let's see what we have."

He did.

She had to force herself not to wince when she saw the tooth. Almost half of it was missing. It must have hurt like hell. "You did a number on that molar, all right. It needs a crown."

"What does that entail?"

"Well, first I'll anesthetize the tooth—"

"With a needle?"

"Jeff, you're not afraid of needles, are you?"

He didn't answer.

She tried not to giggle as she assembled more tools, more paraphernalia for the tedious task ahead.

"Hey, it's not nice to make fun of people's fears. I seem to recall a certain dentist who acted like a big baby when I wanted to clean up a few scrapes on her leg."

Allison remembered that day as if it had just happened. She hadn't been afraid of the first aid; she'd been tense at the idea of Jeff touching her, because she'd been worried she would somehow reveal her secret longing for him. That was in the presex days, when life had been simpler.

But she wouldn't go back there. Painful as it had been, she was glad she'd taken the risk with Jeff. She had beautiful memories, and she was optimistic they would someday be able to restore their friendship. When she stopped aching every time she looked at him. In a hundred years or so.

When Allison tried to give Jeff the anesthetic, he almost bit down on the needle.

"Am I going to have to gas you?" she asked impatiently.

He looked hopeful. "You have nitrous oxide?"

"Only for the real cowards."

"That's me."

In moments she had him connected to the gas via a tube that rested under his nose.

When she judged he was relaxed enough, she stuck the syringe in his mouth and administered the anesthetic. He didn't even flinch.

This close to him, she could smell his skin and the faint scent of his shampoo and soap. It made her mouth water.

"I can't feel my face," he said a few minutes later.

"You're not supposed to. Jeez, Jeff, did you cut class the day they taught you about anesthetics?"

"I sound like my mouth's full of cotton."

"Then maybe it would be better if you just didn't try to talk."

"But I have to. This might be my only chance. I have things to tell you—important things."

"These really aren't the ideal circumstances under which to discuss important things," she said, knowing it was the nitrous oxide loosening his tongue. "Open up, please."

She took an X-ray of the broken tooth, then left the room to develop it, taking advantage of the time to pull herself together. Why was he doing this to her? She'd made up her mind that she would survive without Jeff. Now he was saying things that made irrational hope flare up in her heart.

"Good news," she said breezily as she reentered the treatment room. "There's no sign of decay. I'll just smooth off the rough edges, then put on a temporary crown. In a week or so, you can come back for the porcelain crown."

He gave her a dopey grin.

"Why do you have to be so damn sexy?" she murmured as she changed the tip on her drill.

"What?"

"Nothing. Open up. Let me know if you feel any pain."

"I feel pain every day I'm without you."

"Oh, you silver-tongued devil. Open *up*, please. I haven't got all day."

Chapter Fourteen

As she worked, Allison's professionalism took over, and she forgot, or at least was able to overlook, her proximity to Jeff. He closed his eyes while she reshaped his damaged tooth.

But the moment she finished rinsing his mouth, he started in on her again.

"I'm totally in love with you, you know," he continued relentlessly, as if there'd never been a pause in the conversation. "Why do you think I moved heaven and earth to find you when you were in the hospital?"

She thought about that as she prepared the dental stone for the impression of Jeff's tooth. It was extraordinary, the effort he'd made to find her.

And maybe he did love her, in his own way. But not unconditionally. It had not escaped her attention that all this lovey-dovey stuff was coming out of his mouth only *after* she'd gotten a clean bill of health.

"You're a very...concerned friend, Jeff, and I appreciate it. I'm sorry I refused to see you at the hospital. I know that wasn't very gracious of me. Open up.''

He did, but something in his eyes told her he wasn't finished, that he still had a point to make.

The moment she removed the mold, he tried again. "You have to listen, Allison. I love you. I want you to bear my children.''

Allison nearly collapsed against the work counter. Why did he have to mention children? *He's under the influence of a drug,* she reminded herself. *He's not in his right mind.* People said all kinds of crazy things when they were on laughing gas. He was probably going to faint from embarrassment later.

''I love you, too, Jeff,'' she said evenly as she prepared the medium she would use to make the temporary crown. ''I've always wanted to name my first child after you, anyway. Jughead Hardison.''

''Jughead. Well, okay, if you say so. Oh, of course there'd be a wedding first.''

''Of course.'' She steeled herself, then turned back toward him. ''We can talk about this later, okay? Open up.''

The hurt expression on his face almost did her in. Somehow, though, she managed to finish putting on the temporary crown without further incident.

''All done. I want you to rest here for a few minutes till the effects of the gas wear off.'' *And, please, forget everything we talked about while you're at it.*

She slipped into her office to prepare a bill. Normally she would have let him have the dental work free—professional courtesy. But after the hell he'd put her through over the past hour, she figured he owed her.

JEFF LAY in the dentist's chair, feeling frustrated and dazed and not quite knowing why.

The procedure had been painless in more ways than one. It seemed only a few minutes ago that he'd been sitting here arguing with Allison about needles, and she'd made the welcome suggestion about nitrous oxide. But a look at his watch confirmed he'd been here over an hour.

The laughing gas had relaxed him, all right. He hardly remembered anything of the last hour. Except...Allison had gotten angry with him for some reason. With his inhibitions suppressed, had he made some inappropriate suggestion? Had he done something worse, like grope her?

He sat up, finding his head clear—not even a trace effect of the drug. He felt completely like himself, except for some numbness around his mouth.

He stood and went in search of Allison, who had to be around here somewhere. She wouldn't just leave him here alone. He found her sitting at the receptionist's desk doing paperwork.

She jumped when he called her name. "Oh, Jeff. How do you feel?"

"Fine, physically. Mentally I'm a little muddled. What do I owe you?" He reached for his wallet.

"Oh, don't worry about it." She crumpled up the piece of paper she'd been working on, which he realized was a tally for his bill. "I was going to charge you for being such a pain in the butt, but that would be petty."

A pain in the butt? "Allison, what did I do? I'm afraid I don't remember."

"You don't remember?"

"Nothing, except…well, I think you were mad at me."

She gave him a bittersweet smile. The sadness in her eyes was almost palpable. "You didn't say anything wrong."

"Then what?"

"Nothing! Just leave, please?"

So much for his big plans to use the dental emergency to his advantage. Now didn't seem to be the best time to talk, not after he'd somehow offended her.

He found his jacket, shrugged it on and headed for the door. He had no car, but it was a good day for walking off his frustration. He opened the door, but instead of walking through it, he let it close again.

Oh, cripes, it was all coming back to him. He'd told Allison he loved her. He'd proposed to her—again. And she'd blown him off. But that was because she'd assumed he hadn't been in his right mind.

Damn it, he'd meant every word! Maybe he hadn't spoken as eloquently as he would have liked, but he'd been speaking the complete truth.

He stood poised with his hand on the door, debating whether he should go back and set the record straight. It might be a refreshing change of pace for him to declare his feelings when neither of them was under the influence of a mind-altering drug.

He heard a sob coming from Allison's direction. Oh, hell, he'd made her cry. The urge to flee was almost overwhelming. But the urge to make things right with Allison was stronger. Resolutely he turned and headed back to the receptionist's area. The door was open, so she didn't realize he'd returned until he was standing right by her side.

She jumped, then quickly tried to disguise the fact she was crying. "Jeff! I thought you'd left." She rubbed under her eyes with the heels of her hands.

He grasped her by the shoulders and pulled her out of her chair, holding her so that she was nose to nose with him, and so she couldn't escape.

"Jeff, what are you—"

"You listen to me, Allison Crane. I love you. I was completely stupid before for not telling you how much you mean to me. You were right, I was afraid to commit. I walked away first because I didn't want to be the one left behind." The words poured out of him like oil from a gusher, and Allison's eyes just got bigger and bigger. "But I know now that loving you is worth the risk, any risk. I want to marry you. And I'm going to keep asking until I get the answer I want. Oh, and one other thing. Jughead is not an appropriate name for our firstborn."

"No?" she squeaked.

"I remember every word I said over the past hour,

and I meant every word, too. Just like I meant everything I said at the hospital. But you don't believe—''

''What do you mean, 'at the hospital'?''

''You know, at the hospital. Before your surgery.''

''We never talked before my surgery. You didn't even get there until I was in the operating room.''

''Yes, I did. I used my doctor credentials to get into preop. Are you telling me you don't remember it? Any of it?''

''I was shot up with Demerol!'' He released his death grip on her arms, and she sank back into her chair. ''I had a dream about you, though. This real sappy dream where you said...and you gave me a—'' She gasped. ''Did you give me a ring?''

He nodded, smiling slowly. Finally she was getting it.

''Was it an oval, about two carats, with smaller diamonds all around it?''

He nodded.

''Oh, my God, what did you pay for it?''

''What? Why do you want to know that? It's my grandmother's ring.''

Allison put a hand over her mouth, horrified. ''I lost it. I lost your grandmother's ring, a family heirloom,'' she said in despair. ''I didn't recognize it, and I told the nurse it wasn't mine!'' She sprang out of the chair and threw her arms around him, crying now in earnest. ''Oh, Jeff, you...gave me a ring, a beautiful ring—*before* the surgery—and I...lost it.''

"I don't care about the ring," he soothed. "I care about the words that went with it. I asked you to marry me. In fact, I've asked several times now. And as I recall, you haven't given me an answer."

She was saying something, but she was crying so hard, and with her face muffled against his jacket, he couldn't understand a word.

"Allie, baby, don't cry. Please, please."

She pulled away so he could hear her. "I always cry when I'm happy."

"Is that a yes?"

"Yes!" She tried to kiss him, but with his mouth still numb the effect was less than satisfactory.

"Can I take a rain check on that kiss?" he asked.

She laughed through her tears of joy. "Okay. First thing, though, when your mouth wakes up. And maybe the second thing and the third thing, too. Every day for the rest of our lives."

"Our long, long lives," he added.

Abruptly she let go of him and grabbed her purse from the desk drawer where she kept it. "I have to go."

"Now? Where?"

She turned to him. "I'm driving to Dallas, to the hospital, to get my ring back!" Then she started switching off lights.

"Well, hold your horses, I'm coming with you."

SUNDAY DINNER at the Hardison Ranch was an event to remember. Jeff invited Allison's parents, and the happy couple made a formal announcement concerning their upcoming nuptials.

"Well, it's about time," Anne said as everyone made a toast with the beverages that happened to be on the table, which included lemonade, iced tea, milk and water. "I've never seen two such blind, stubborn people."

"Oh, I don't know about that," Jeff argued. "I seem to recall a certain stubborn redhead and my bullheaded little brother—"

"Let's not go there," Wade interrupted. "Ancient history."

"What is it they say about the course of true love?" Sally asked, casting a sidelong look at Pete. Then she turned to Allison. "Now, let me have a closer look at that gorgeous rock on your hand, young lady."

"It's your turn now, Daddy," Kristin piped up.

Jonathan looked startled. "What?"

"Well, first Uncle Wade got married to Anne, and now Uncle Jeff is getting married to Allison. So it's your turn."

Everyone laughed, and Allison murmured to Jeff, "Out of the mouths of babes."

"That'll be the day," Pete said. "Jon's too ornery to get married again."

Ed pointed his fork at Pete. "Seems to me we always said that about you."

Pete grumbled something under his breath. His own nuptials with Sally were fast approaching, and he didn't like being reminded of his romantic side. It upset his grumpy-old-man image.

Jeff enjoyed the good-natured squabbling. He enjoyed the whole dinner, and he hoped there would be many more. He looked forward to adding more chairs to the table as he and Allison produced new cousins for Kristin, Sam and Olivia.

He knew fate could come in at any time and upset his optimistic view of the future, but he was no longer afraid. Every life was made up of joys and sorrows, large and small. The sorrows were what made the joys so wondrous. Having known loneliness made him savor the love and companionship he'd so recently found with Allison.

He'd learned not to let fears of the unknown spoil what he had right here, right now. His love for Allison had been like a tight bud inside his heart, afraid to open. Now it was in full bloom—a whole garden of blooms—and he intended to savor every day with her as a special gift for as long as they lived.

* * * * *

Yup. You guessed it. Jonathan's story is next. But you'll never believe which lady is going to marry this Hardison. Watch for

SASSY CINDERELLA

coming from Harlequin American Romance in December 2002.

Beginning in October from

TRADING PLACES

**A brand-new duo from
popular Harlequin authors**

RITA HERRON
and
DEBRA WEBB

**When identical twin brothers decide to trade lives,
they get much more than they bargained for!**

Available October 2002

THE RANCHER WORE SUITS
by Rita Herron
Rugged rancher Ty Cooper uses his down-home
charms to woo beautiful pediatrician Jessica.

Available November 2002

THE DOCTOR WORE BOOTS
by Debra Webb
Ty's next-door neighbor Leanne finds herself falling for
sophisticated and sexy Dr. Dex Montgomery.

Available at your favorite retail outlet.

Makes any time special ®